THEATRE ROYAL STRATFORD EAST *...a people's theatre*

8th July – 29th July

Theatre Royal Stratford East presents the world premiere of

summer in london

by Rikki Beadle-Blair

First performed at Theatre Royal Stratford East on
Saturday 8th July 2017

Published June 2017 by Team Angelica Publishing,
an imprint of Angelica Entertainments Ltd

Team Angelica Publishing
51 Coningham Road
London W12 8BS

TEAM
ANGELICA

www.teamangelica.com

A CIP catalogue record for this book is available from
the British Library

ISBN 978-0-9955162-2-9

Printed and bound by Lightning Source

Credits

Cast (in alphabetical order):

Jack **Ash Palmisciano**
Justine **Emma Frankland**
Ryoko **Kamari Romeo**
Joan **Mzz Kimberley**
Mosey **Tigger Blaize**
Hamza **Tyler Luke Cunningham**
Summer **Victoria Gigante**

Creative team:

Writer and Director **Rikki Beadle-Blair**
Set Designer **Tom Paris**
Costume Designer **Jonathan Lipman**
Lighting Designer **Jack Weir**
Sound Designer **Chris Murray**
Assistant Director **Sarah Meadows**

Production credits:

Production Manager **Richard Parr**
Costume Supervisor **Kitty Hawkins**
Company & Stage Manager **Sarah Buik**
Deputy Stage Manager **Marie Costa**
Assistant Stage Manager **Stephen Freeman**
Head of Lighting **Laura Curd**
Head of Sound **Chris Murray**
Head of Stage **Guy Fryer**
Wardrobe Manager **Mike Lees**
Costume Assistant **TJ Howes**
Technical Apprentice **Deanna Towli**

Costume Supplier **Angels Costume London**
Artwork design **Rebecca Pitt**
Promotional videos **Mann Bros**
Production photography **Sharron Wallace**
Set builders **Leviathan Workshop**

Writer and Director

Rikki Beadle-Blair is a writer, director, composer, choreographer, designer, producer and performer. He has won several awards including the Sony Award, the Los Angeles Outfest Screenwriting Award, and was ranked forth on the Rainbow list of the UK's hundred most influential LGBT+ people. Beadle-Blair works extensively in theatre and has written 28 plays in the last decade that have been performed at Theatre Royal Stratford East, Bush Theatre, Soho Theatre, Tristan Bates Theatre and Contact Theatre in Manchester. For television and film his credits include BLACKBIRD starring Oscar-winning actress Mo'nique, STONEWALL, METRO-SEXUALITY, NOAH'S ARC; and FIT, KICKOFF and BASHMENT for his company Team Angelica. He is also one of the creative directors of the Visionary Youth Project for Young European Film Activists. If you want to work with Rikki write to rikki@teamangelica.com

Set Designer

Tom Paris trained at the Royal Welsh College of Music & Drama. Design Credits: SUMMER IN LONDON (Theatre Royal Stratford East), JUDY! (West End), ENTER WONDER.LAND (National Theatre), SAXON COURT (Southwark Playhouse), ALICE (Salisbury Playhouse), NOYE'S FLUDDE (Iford Arts/ Salisbury Playhouse), ALICE IN WONDERLAND (Greenwich

Theatre), FAUST, CARMEN, THE MARRIAGE OF FIGARO, THE ELIXIR OF LOVE (Winterbourne Opera), INTO THE WOODS (Lowry Theatre), MACK & MABEL (Greenwich Theatre), HIS DARK MATERIALS (Sixth Sense), ANYTHING GOES, EVITA (Musical Theatre Salisbury), HELLO AGAIN (RWCMD), THE LONDON CUCKOLDS (Chapter Arts Centre)

Design Associate to Rae Smith: WONDER.LAND (National Theatre/M.I.F./Chatalet), CAVALLERIA RUSTICANA and PAGLIACCI (Metropolitan Opera), THE TEMPEST (Birmingham Royal Ballet), THE MODERATE SOPRANO (Hampstead), PELLÉAS ET MÉLISANDE (Scottish Opera), and THE LION THE WITCH & THE WARDROBE (West Yorkshire Playhouse)

Tom has worked as a design assistant in the West End and internationally with designers Katrina Lindsay, Rob Howell, Robert Jones, Bob Crowley, Hildegard Bechtler and David Farley. www.tomparis.co.uk

Costume Designer

Jonathan Lipman: As Costume Designer: THE BRAILLE LEGACY, DEATH TAKES A HOLIDAY, RAGTIME, IN THE BAR OF A TOKYO HOTEL, THE MIKADO (Charing Cross); ALLEGRO, GREY GARDENS (Southwark Playhouse); MURDER IN THE CATHEDRAL (Middle Temple); THE COUNTRY GIRL, KEELER (West End & UK tours); LARKRISE TO CANDLEFORD, THE HAUNTING, JEKYLL AND HYDE: THE MUSICAL, BLOCKBUSTER: THE MUSICAL (UK tours); LA FANCIULLA DEL WEST, UN BALLO IN MASCHERA, DIE FLEDERMAUS (Opera Up Close, Kings Head); TOSCA, LA TRAVIATA (Opera Up Close, Kings Head, UK tours & West End); VIEUX CARRE (Theatre Up Close, Kings Head & West End); THE HANDYMAN (Yvonne Arnaud & UK tour); QUASIMODO, A TALE OF TWO CITIES (Theatre Up Close, Kings Head); POPE JOAN (NYT).

As Associate Costume Designer: RICHARD III (Old Vic, BAM & world tour); DR DEE (Manchester Int. Festival & ENO). www.jonathanlipman.co.uk

Lighting Designer

Jack Weir trained at the Guildhall School and was presented with the ETC award for lighting design in 2014. In 2016 he was nominated for a WhatsOnStage Award for Best Lighting Design on THE BOYS IN THE BAND (Vaudeville Theatre, West End). He was also double-nominated and a finalist in the 2016 Off West End Awards for Best Lighting Designer. Some of his work includes: JUDY! (Arts, West End); BETTY BLUE EYES (Chichester Uni); THE PLAGUE (The Arcola); CAT! – THE PLAY (Ambassadors Theatre); ASSATA TAUGHT ME (The Gate); RAY COONEY'S OUT OF ORDER (Yvonne Arnaud & UK Tour); LA RONDE (The Bunker); PRAY SO HARD FOR YOU (The Finborough); THE BOYS IN THE BAND (West End, Park Theatre & UK Tour); CONFESSIONAL, THROUGH THE MILL (Southwark Playhouse); NO VILLAIN (Trafalgar Studios); LITTLE VOICE (The Union Theatre); THE LIFE (University of Chichester); PRINCESS CARABOO (Finborough Theatre); FOUR PLAY (Theatre503); AFRICAN GOTHIC (The Park Theatre); NO VILLAIN (Old Red Lion Theatre); MY CHILDREN! MY AFRICA! (Trafalgar Studios); MUSWELL HILL (Park Theatre); BAD GIRLS, ROAD SHOW, FEAR & MISERY and THE SPITFIRE GRILL (The Union Theatre); ALL-MALE PIRATES OF PENZANCE (UK Tour). www.weirdlighting.co.uk

Sound Designer

Chris Murray is the Head of Sound at Theatre Royal Stratford East. Previous design work includes: COUNTING STARS, LOVE

'N' STUFF (Theatre Royal Stratford East), WRETCH (Mercury Theatre Colchester & Edinburgh Fringe Festival). THE CAUCASIAN CHALK CIRCLE, THE KITCHEN, NORA – A DOLL'S HOUSE and STOCKHOLM (Mercury Theatre Colchester).

Assistant Director

Sarah Meadows was recently nominated for Best Director, by Off West End Awards 2016 for SCREWED by Kathryn O'Reilly.

Recent credits include: Associate Director, THE REAL THING by Tom Stoppard, directed by Stephen Unwin, UK tour (including Cambridge Arts Theatre, The Rose Kingston, Bath Theatre Royal); ON THE CREST OF A WAVE, Camilla Whitehill & Longsight Theatre, VAULT Festival; THE TEXAS TAXMAN (musical comedy), Luke Courtier, The Arcola, VAULT Festival, RADA festival; WHERE DO LITTLE BIRDS GO? by Camilla Whitehill, Old Red Lion, UK tour, VAULT Festival & Edinburgh Festival, Underbelly; ILE LA WA by Tolu Agbelusi & Apples & Snakes, Contact Theatre, Rich Mix; SCREWED by Kathryn O'Reilly, Theatre 503; THE VERY PERRY SHOW (comedy) by Kate Perry, San Francisco International Arts Festival;); MR INCREDIBLE by Camilla Whitehill, VAULT Festival & Edinburgh Festival; YOU by Mark Wilson, Brighton Festival, VAULT Festival (UK tour). In development; THE FEAR OF FEAR by Stephanie Ridings in collaboration with Warwick Arts Centre.

Sarah is represented by Colin Blumenau at The Production Exchange Management.

Cast (in alphabetical order)

Tigger Blaize (MOSEY) returns to Theatre Royal Stratford East to play Mosey – previous work for the company includes SUPER SKINNY BITCHES. Theatre credits include INTERTWINED (Bush Theatre), THE ELVES AND THE SHOEMAKERS (Theatre Hullabaloo), SPOT'S BIRTHDAY PARTY (Oxford Playhouse, UK tour), RABBIT & HEDGEHOG (York Theatre Royal), THE TWITS (Belgrade Theatre Coventry, UK tour). TV credits include APPLE TREE YARD, and the forthcoming HARD SUN.

Mzz Kimberley (JOAN) Theatre credits include THE MAIDS (Russian tour), THE LAS VEGAS STORY, IN THE FLESH (world tour), THE VAMPIRES OF SODOM (New York) and TRANS SCRIPTS (UK tour). TV credits include WAVE LENGTHS and COLD FEET. Film credits include KILLER TONGUE and PREACHING TO THE PERVERTED. Kimberley is also one of the leads in new web series SPECTRUM LONDON.

Tyler Luke Cunningham (HAMZA) This production marks his stage debut. TV credits include BOY MEETS GIRL.

Emma Frankland (JUSTINE) An award-winning theatre maker and performer (two-time Fringe First award winner and Total Theatre Award nominee), her work include NONE OF US IS YET A ROBOT, RITUALS FOR CHANGE and DON QUIJOTE (British Council Showcase at Edinburgh Fringe, UK & international tour). She is also an Associate Artist with Coney and Chisenhale Dance Space.

Victoria Gigante (SUMMER) Theatre credits include RISE (Waterloo Green) and MY DAD'S GAY YEAR (Bush Theatre).

Ash Palmisciano (JACK) Theatre credits include KING LEAR (RSC). TV credits include BOY MEETS GIRL and MUM

Kamari Romeo (RYOKO) Theatre credits include THE BEAR/THE PROPOSAL (Young Vic), ELEMENTAL (Bush Theatre), SEQUIN DEEP (Theatre N16), THE JUNGLE BOOK (Emporium Brighton) and ALICE IN WONDERLAND (The Minack Theatre).

Special thanks to:

Rachel George, Rachel Goldsmith, Estelle Cleary, Richard Green, Holly Martin and Preece Killick
Milestone Leisure Limited
Sister Flowers limited
Jackson Leisure Supplies www.jacksonsleisure.com
Blukoo Limited www.blukoo.com
Polybags limited www.polybags.co.uk
Vape Club www.vapeclub.co.uk
Simply Eliquid www.simplyeliquid.co.uk
Team Angelica Publishing: John R Gordon, Carleen Beadle, Rikki Beadle-Blair, Collin Clay Chase www.teamangelica.com

Foreword

Every project is an epic adventure and working on *Summer in London* has turned out to be especially epic.

It was a year ago when I fell in love with the idea of creating a play with an all trans cast. I was excited by the idea of creating a world in which a perceived minority was the majority. No coming out, no confessions, no 'I've got something to tell you...' Kerry Michael, the brave, bold artistic director of one of the world's bravest, boldest, most welcoming theatres, Theatre Royal Stratford East, was, as always, an enthusiastic collaborator.

Since I was a kid I've always preferred to cast first and then write for the actors. Not so I can write about them specifically: I'm not trying to write their biographies. Nor is this a devising/co-writing process. Instead we sit round a table for a few sessions and we talk about anything and everything that comes to mind. Sometimes, if I already know the themes of the play, we discuss those, and often have moral and ethical discussions/arguments. That's all valuable, and a lot of the random or pertinent things we discuss appear in the final script, but it's more general inspiration I'm searching for. I'm absorbing the vibe of the room, the chemistry between the participants – taking samples of their DNA and mixing it with mine. Trying to make a baby that looks a bit like them and a bit like me, but is ultimately its own thing.

It's an odd process to explain. Rather like being a fashion designer and creating a collection with a set of models in mind. Just as Kate Moss might never wear the designs she models in fashion shows in her daily life, but rocks them with a sense of ownership on the runway or in the photoshoot, the characters I create for my casts to inhabit are created with them in mind, but are not necessarily representative of them – though hopefully they fit like a glove. And hopefully the cast are just comfortable enough, and just challenged enough, to make this a rewarding and exciting experience for them, me, and ultimately the audience.

While starting the process of meetings with potential actors I was still looking for a theme. Last year there was a July heatwave, and one night I noticed how many couples were out after dark in the parks and along canals and the riverside, and how they blended with the homeless people, also conducting their own courtships and romances... and that sparked the idea for the play and the title. I really wanted to create something romantic, and what could be more romantic than summer in London? That random time of the year when we forget that we are in England and everyone gets glowing and sexy, and smiles. And so much to do for free! Winter is long and depressing – especially for the homeless – but every summer – when we get one... feels like a Summer of Love.

Once I had found my family/team (I could have cast the show at least three times over with the wonderful people I met) we started the table meetings. And then the adventure really began. The discussions were impassioned and intense and soooo uplifting. It was fantastic to be in a room with such a diverse group of people who were elated at being the majority. Swept up in their joy, honesty, strength, enthusiasm, laughter and kinship I left every workshop feeling so involved and so full of my company that I would have to shake myself and remind myself that I was not trans. And I realised that was the gift I wanted to give the audience. Besides entertainment. The gift of community. I suspect that's always been my goal with everything I've ever worked on.

People ask me, 'Why an all-trans cast for this show's first production?' After all, the word trans is never mentioned. The obvious answer is why not? Why shouldn't a story be told from an entirely trans point of view? Why shouldn't they have universal stories to tell? Why shouldn't they lead the way? More and more I realise that we are all trans, each of us exploring our identities as men or women, exploring the borders of our masculinity and femininity, our maleness and femaleness, and inhabiting our bodies in our own way, both privately and publicly. Who has never had a tiny moment of gender crisis? Fretting about how we come across, wondering how we stack up against others, trying not to disappoint our parents or alienate our peers, or alternatively, busting out in defiance of what's expected of us? I happen to think that people who are brave enough to claim and explore their trans identities are like astronauts – people who are willing to visit the fringes of what is within reach, and leave their footsteps and our flags in places the rest of us have only dared dream of exploring.

Of course many lines and moments take on a particular resonance when one knows that the character is trans. Just as they would if the cast were all women, or all gay, or all Scottish or all deaf or all Jamaican. I hope I get to see the play performed by all kinds of groups and all kinds of mixtures. But if anyone ever performs *Summer in London* in the future, please remember: you are walking in the footsteps of some brilliant, brave and very beautiful cosmonauts. Please honour them with your own version of courage.

Rikki Beadle-Blair

THEATRE ROYAL STRATFORD EAST ...*a people's theatre*

Administration and Operations
Executive Director Deborah Sawyerr
Building and Facilities Manager Graeme Bright
Building Maintenance Person Pravie Maharaj
IT Systems Manager Stuart Saunders
Operations Coordinator Velma Fontaine
Building and Maintenance Assistant Myles Eugene
General Manager Wendy Dempsey

Archives
Mary Ling
Murray Melvin

Artistic
Producer Bella Rodrigues
Gerry's Associate Producer Daisy Hale
Associate Producer Karen Fisher
Agent For Change (Ramps On The Moon) Kate Lovell
Artistic Director Kerry Michael
Associate Director Pooja Ghai
Assistant to Artistic Director Rita Mishra
Musical Theatre New Writing Manager Sevan Tavoukdjian

Artistic Associates
Associate Artist in Residence Simon Startin
Associate Artists
Cosh Omar
Daniel Bailey
Marcus Romer
Martina Laird
Ola Ince
Rani Moorthy
Simielia Hodge-Dallaway
ULTZ
Associate Companies
Artistic Directors of the Future (ADF)
Team Angelica
International Associates
Fred Carl (USA)

Rob Lee (USA)

Companies in Partnership
Ballet Black
New Musical Development Collective (NMDC)
Writer in Residence Atiha Sen Gupta

Bar and Catering Staff
Head of Bars and Catering Ian Williams
Duty Manager Laurie Anderson, Iuliana Toma
Bars Manager Marcin Zawistowski
Bar Team Leaders Azuka Essu-Taylor, Unique Spencer
Agne Vilkaite, Bianca Jade Lowe-Vidal, Cartell Ashley Lowe-Vidal, Dorota Bukowska,
Dwain Innis, Dylan Ward, Kellie Murphy, Lauren Moore, Luke Simpson, Luke Dash,
Rachel Pierre, Robert Eames, Tom Dale
Theatre Workshop Bar Staff Andrea Leprini, Audrey Marie Matthews, Cartell Ashley
Lowe-Vidal, Khari Palmer-Harris, Manasha Mudhir, Nduaya Ilunga, Roma Grisanovaite,
Sydney Weise
Gerrys' Staff Agne Vilkaite, Michela Lettieri, Mihaela Opera, Nareg Derkeshishian,
Pamela Galasso, Sara Meloni **(Team Leader)**, Jack Murphy, Holly Weaver

Box Office
Angela Frost **(Box Office Manager)**
Amaryllis Courtney, Asha Bhatti, Beryl Warner **(Box Office Supervisor)**, Julie Lee, Karen
Whyte and Russeni Fisher.

Development
Development Administrator Cat March
Development Officer Chris Alexander
Director of Development & Communications Sal Goldsmith

Domestic Assistants
Cosimo Cupello, Manjit Kaur Babbra, Marjorie Walcott, Nasima Akhtar Shelly, Sydney
Weise

Finance
Finance Officer (temporary cover) Ben Beever
Head of Finance Jane Kortlandt
Finance Officer Sibhat Kesete
Finance Officer Titilayo Onanuga

Front of House
Russeni Fisher **(Front of House Manager)**
Alan Bailey **(Head Usher)**,Alex Jarrett, Alex Uzoka, Anita Brown, Caroline Wilson **(Head
Usher)**,Charlotte West, Charly Smith, Danielle Hilaire, Elsie Frangou, Emily Usher, Erin
Read, Itoya Osagiede, Jack Matthews, **(Head Usher)**, Jamaal Norman **(Fire Marshal)**,
Jessica Kennedy, Karina Ginola, Leeam Francis **(Head Usher)**, Lucy Harrigan **(Head
Usher)**, Myles Jeremiah-Best **(Duty Manager)**, Miguel Powell, Robert Eames **(Head
Usher)**, Rose-Marie Christian **(Duty Manager)**, Roymere Lowe-Vidal, Tiana Gravillis.

THEATRE ROYAL STRATFORD EAST ...a people's theatre

This famous producing theatre, located in the heart of London's East End prides itself on creating world class work that reflects the concerns, hopes and dreams of its community. A prolific developer of new work, this award-winning theatre attracts artists and audiences who are often not represented in other venues, and it is firmly committed to supporting the development of exciting new voices and bold new work.

Recently staged new productions include the world premiere of Room, Atiha Sen Gupta's *Counting Stars*, Kirsten Childs' *The Bubbly Black Girl Sheds Her Chameleon Skin*, Bonnie Greer's *The Hotel Cerise* and the Ramps On The Moon production of The Who's *Tommy* directed by our Artistic Director Kerry Michael.

Contact Us
Theatre Royal Stratford East
Gerry Raffles Square
London E15 1BN

Box Office & Information
020 8534 0310 Mon-Sat, 10am-6pm
www.stratfordeast.com
theatreroyal@stratfordeast.com

Twitter	@stratfordeast
Facebook	/theatreroyalstratfordeast
Typetalk	07972 918 050
Administration	020 8534 7374

Registration Number 556251
Charity Number 233801
VAT Number 233 3120 59

SUPPORT OUR WORK AS A REGISTERED CHARITY

As a registered charity the support of individuals, business partners and charitable trusts is vital. By choosing to become a member of our Vision Collective or by making a donation, you will assist us in keeping ticket prices affordable for our community. You will also help to ensure we can continue our work with young people, many of whom are not in education or employment.

For more information or a chat, please contact our Development Team on 0208 2791105 or email development@stratfordeast.com.

Supported using public funding by
ARTS COUNCIL ENGLAND   Newham London

WE WOULD LIKE TO THANK THE FOLLOWING FOR THEIR SUPPORT

MAJOR DONORS
Scrutton Estates Ltd
The Sahara Care Charitable Trust

VISION COLLECTIVE
Pioneers Andrew Cowan, Angela & Stephen Jordan, Ed Ross, Elizabeth & Derek Joseph, The Hearn Foundation, Hilary and Stuart Williams, Kerry Michael, Nigel Farnall & Angelica Puscasu, Sabine Vinck, Tim Bull & Rosalind Riley, Trevor Williams and all those who wish to remain anonymous

Directors Collective Hedley G. Wright, Rachel Potts for Jon Potts, and all those who wish to remain anonymous

BUSINESS SUPPORTERS
Bloomberg, Devonshires Solicitors, Galliard Homes and Telford Homes

TRUSTS AND FOUNDATIONS
Achates Philanthropy Foundation, Allan & Nesta Ferguson Charitable Trust, Aspers Good Causes Fund, The Aviva Community Foundation, The D'Oyly Carte Charitable Trust, Esmée Fairbairn Foundation, The Goldsmiths' Company, Jack Petchey Foundation, The Leche Trust, The Mackintosh Foundation, The Newham Giving Fund, The Rank Foundation, The Robert Gavron Trust, Trust for London and Worshipful Company of Basketmakers 2011 Charitable Trust

We would also like to acknowledge the generous support of the Monument Trust

Rikki Beadle-Blair

summer in london

TEAM
ANGELICA

CAST

HAMZA – seeks safety in cynicism

RYOKO – wounded child

MOSEY – weary optimist

JACK – wannabe romantic

JUSTINE – awkwardly enchanting

JOAN – poised and powerful

SUMMER – sweetly devastatingly innocently honest

FULL MOON OVER OLYMPIC PARK

The ghost of SUMMER'S SMILE flickers across the moon's surface.

She laughs...

HAMZA, tangled in his silver blanket, awakes with a start.

HAMZA: Aaah!

Caught in a shaft of moonlight, HAMZA stares around him.

HAMZA: (CONT'D) Oh man... Not this crap again. Man's trying to get some rest!

HAMZA lies back down.

SUMMER MOON laughs again, flirtily.

HAMZA: (CONT'D) You know what... just shut up.

HAMZA lies down again...

SUMMER MOON laughs once again.

HAMZA hurls his shoe at the moon. It shatters like a chandelier and all the lights go out...

Blackness.

HAMZA: (CONT'D) Oooops.

Then out come the stars... HAMZA sits up and looks.

HAMZA: (CONT'D) Okay. You win... For now.

HAMZA sits up watching the stars, until...

THE DAWN...

Then...

SUNRISE

THREE BOYS surround HAMZA under silver blankets, sleeping soundly in the trees. The first rays of sunlight hit them.

JACK'S CLOCK RADIO ALARM rings. HAMZA quickly lies back feigning sleep as JACK, RYOKO and MOSEY stir, moaning.

BOYS: Uhhhhhhh!

JACK drops the CLOCK RADIO, snatches at it, but knocks it away into the grass as it bursts into breakfast banter and song.

DJ: Goooood morning Londooooon!

THE BOYS stretch like cats.

RYOKO: Good morning London!

THE BOYS sit up on their branches in their slightly dishev-elled suits. MOSEY pulls out a pack of wet-wipes and they start wiping their faces and underarms.

MOSEY: Another record-breaking summer morning in the City of Dreams.

HAMZA: It's already 26 degrees Celsius, 79 degrees Fahren-heit and climbing,

JACK: Highs of 33 and 90 are predicted along with clear skies and zero chance of rainfall.

RYOKO: Too hot to stay in bed.

MOSEY: Too hot to go to school.

HAMZA: And definitely too hot to look for a job.

MOSEY: Which on the latest mysteriously perfect summer's day...

HAMZA: ...in the capital of changeable skies...

RYOKO: ...and infinite shades of grey...

JACK: ...Leaves just one question!

RYOKO: What else are you gonna do with it...?

BOYS: Except dance!

THE BOYS dance, straightening out their slightly crumpled suits and ties, and have fun spitting lyrics:

RYOKO: Summertime and it's time to get live
   London town buzzing like a beehive
   East to West End, North to South side
   Every gal on road is my size

JACK: Every cross road, every postcode
   Where the Thames flows
   Wherever you go
   You dun know
   Every garden grows
   London Rose
   In every colour yo.

BOYS: Home!

MOSEY: She is the empire legacy

BOYS: Home!

MOSEY: The pretty girl sat next to me

BOYS: Home!

MOSEY: On the tube on the bus on the DLR to South Quay

BOYS: Home!

MOSEY: Only friends no enemies

BOYS: Home!

MOSEY: This weather brings out the best in me

BOYS: Home

MOSEY: London stole my heart, now summer's come for the rest of me

HAMZA: All you dudes hanging out pon road
   Gangsta hoodies in bad man clothes
   Slaves in chains made of white gold
   Boy betta know
   You're just getting old
   All you rude boys swagger pon street
   Dreaming you could step like me
   Float like butterfly sting like bee
   Love Child of Mohammed Ali
   Free!
   Good God Almighty Free at last!

The boys gaze blissfully at the climbing sun in the light of a huge sunrise, staring at the morning reflecting off the glass of CANARY WHARF.

HAMZA: (CONT'D) Who's hungry?

RYOKO: I was born hungry.

JACK: Everyone's born hungry, man.

MOSEY: Guess that's all of us, then.

HAMZA: Guess we should eat then.

They exchange looks.

They spud fists and scatter.

MOSEY: Remember, men – you're hustling for four!

RYOKO: One of all!

ALL FOUR LADS: And all for fun!

JACK approaches a lady in the audience.

JACK: (*Strong Manchester accent*) Alright there, sweetheart, gazing all goggle-eyed at your Google-maps, am I correct in thinking you look a bit... lost? Well, it's your lucky day, darlin' 'cause I'm a Londoner me, was it the accent what gave me away, like?
(*even stronger Manchester*)
Cheeky chappie born right here within the sound of Bow bells! And you – let me hazard a guess – are a Princess Royal of a foreign realm, here on a stately visit and slipped away from your bodyguards to slum it with the common folk. And now you're lost. Well, do not fret, your highness, your humble servant is here to guide you to your destination. (*reacts*)
'Cash'?? Do I look like I care about cash? You can pay me in

smiles, yeah? Or – okay – seeing as I can see you're about to insist – you can buy me a chicken sandwich for breakfast if it makes you happy and we'll call it quits, yeah? Deal? In fact, how about I summon my three besties and we all four of us walk you to the safe-zone as a posse – a security squad of gentleman bodyguards fit for a future queen and all for the price of a bargain bucket of KFC? You what? Sorry – it's hard to concentrate when an accent's that sexy... Sorry, who? (*looking round*) Husband?
(*gutted*)
'Cor blimey', as we say in the manor, He's been eating his Weetabix, ain't he?

As the HUSBAND looms over him...

JACK: (CONT'D) Oiroight Geezer???

JACK runs for his life...

HAMZA approaches a lady in the audience. Sexy-serenades her R. Kelly style.

HAMZA: *Baaaaabeee! Baby Baby Baaaaaaaaaby!*

RYOKO focuses on another lady in the audience.

RYOKO: Oh my days man!

HAMZA: *Now I realise I've been*
 Walking in darkne-e-e-ss,
 But now I see!

RYOKO: You can't do that to a man, sis! Sneaking up on strangers with all that beauty!

HAMZA: *'Cause you, pretty lady,*
  You are the light,
  That shines on me!

RYOKO: Look at me, I'm proper shook.

HAMZA: *You make me wanna be someone good...*

RYOKO: Actually physically trembling.

HAMZA: (*shaking off his hood*) *You make me wanna shake off*
  my hood

RYOKO: Sweating like a cold beer...

HAMZA: *And finally doooooo...*

RYOKO: Positively palpitating!

HAMZA: *...something with this life!*

RYOKO: That's you, babe...

HAMZA: *Be the kind of man who truuuuuly*

RYOKO: ...you know that?

HAMZA: *...honours his wife...*

RYOKO: ...That's you.

HAMZA: *You're just so hard to resist*

RYOKO: I'm actually quite shy, y'know?

HAMZA: *And you know I'm a feminist*

RYOKO: But you – you can change a man.

HAMZA: *Which is why I'm a let ya*
  Buy a bunch of cheeseburgers
  for meeee

RYOKO: Boy, I bet you can <u>COOK!</u> ...innit?!

HAMZA: *And my buddies...*

RYOKO: You're just too perfect not to!

HAMZA: *Wait, surely you ain't leaving?*

RYOKO: Wait, you can't leave me like this!

HAMZA: *Can't you take a lil' teasing?*

RYOKO: All PTSD'd and everyting!

HAMZA: *Please baby don't leave! Don't leave me!*

RYOKO: At least leave me something to remember you by...

HAMZA: *Don't leeeeeaaaave me!*

RYOKO...like some spare change?

HAMZA: *Lonely and hungry and already so deeply... I-i-i- i-*
  iiiiin...

RYOKO: I love you!
  (*forlorn*) Little heartbreaker...
  (*spots next passing girl*)
  Hey baby!

HAMZA: (*Checking out a new girl*) Baaaaabeee!

They follow their respective girls...

RYOKO: Sorry to bother you, but you know, you look like my
  next girlfriend...?

*Someone rushes past HAMZA who stops him in his tracks...
SUMMER.*

*SUDDENLY IT'S NIGHT and the MOON is out and the moon is
laughing SUMMER'S LAUGH.*

BACK TO DAY

Stunned, HAMZA goes after his girl... (not SUMMER)

HAMZA: *Baaaaabeee!*

*JUSTINE stands near a delivery bike for CITYSANDWICHES
.COM. She is feeding birds.*

*MOSEY sneaks up behind JUSTINE, put his hands over her
eyes.*

MOSEY: (*'Sexy' whisper*) Boo!

JUSTINE: No.

MOSEY: Hey, Justine!

JUSTINE: No.

MOSEY: Babe...

JUSTINE: No.

MOSEY: Justine, Babe...

JUSTINE: No.

MOSEY: Why've you gotta be like that?

JUSTINE: No.

MOSEY: You don't know what I'm gonna say.

JUSTINE: No.

MOSEY: You miss me, doncha?

JUSTINE: No.

MOSEY: Still feel me, doncha?

JUSTINE: No.

MOSEY: You want me to go away, doncha?

JUSTINE: No.

 JUSTINE winces.

MOSEY: (*grinning*) Doncha?

JUSTINE: No I don't. I don't want you to go away, 'cause I don't ever want you to come back. I don't want you to piss off. I don't want you to piss me off. I want you to mysteriously vaporize or spontaneously combust or, if it must be tediously scientifically viable, I would be happy for you to drop dead, roll into the street, get struck by a speeding truck, instantly smashed, squashed, shattered and scattered, before being hosed off the tarmac and washed down the sewer. Any more questions? No? Class dismissed.

MOSEY: It's so cute that you so don't mean that.

JUSTINE: Oh, for a moment there I thought I definitely did.

MOSEY: That's just the hormones talking.

JUSTINE: And they're saying up yours.

JUSTINE continues feeding the birds.

MOSEY: You realise that's a violation?

JUSTINE: You're a violation.

MOSEY: You don't even like pigeons. Flying rodents you said. You've changed, Justine.

JUSTINE: What can I say? Turns out I've a soft spot for rats with wings as well as without.

MOSEY: Is that why you're giving 'em white bread with gluten? Such a nature lover. Poisoning pigeons in the park.

JUSTINE: (*holding one out sweetly*) Would you like one?

MOSEY: Yes, please.

JUSTINE: (*snatching it away*) Die screaming, Mosey. Oops, sorry... it's the hormones.

MOSEY: Wow. You are proper stressed from this dead-end job, aincha?

JUSTINE: Thanks for the diagnosis, doc.

MOSEY: You came all this way went through all that shit, battled your way off benefits and out of the back alleys, just to become a pedalling waitress for ShittySandwiches.com.

JUSTINE: I am not a waitress.

MOSEY: What's wrong with being a...

JUSTINE: Nothing. I just don't happen to be one. I'm a travelling sandwich chef.

MOSEY: Is it your boss? Is he giving you grief?

JUSTINE: Mosey...

MOSEY: You need me to sort him out?

JUSTINE: God, no.

MOSEY: I can play the scary geezer.

JUSTINE: No you can't.

MOSEY: I can get proper lary, me. Check out my screw-face.

JUSTINE looks. Looks away, not laughing.

MOSEY: Don't you ever wanna smile again?

JUSTINE: Why waste the energy? I'm over making worthless investments.

MOSEY: Gotta speculate to accumulate, babe!

JUSTINE: If I give you a shitty sandwich will you go away?

MOSEY: Give me four and I'll stay away.

JUSTINE starts making sandwiches.

MOSEY: (CONT'D) Shitty sandwiches are anti-Mosey magnets.

JUSTINE: Like my kisses?

MOSEY: Your kisses ain't shitty. They're surprisingly more-ish.

JUSTINE: How come you never stuck around then?

Silence.

JUSTINE: (CONT'D) No drama. No pressure. Just curiosity.

RYOKO comes running in.

RYOKO: Mosey, man!

JUSTINE: How come you didn't love me?

Sensing the tension, RYOKO swerves out of the way...

RYOKO: (*swerving aside to safety*) Shit!

MOSEY: I don't know. Maybe 'cause you didn't love me.

HAMZA and JACK come running in. RYOKO makes a 'Red Alert' face. They try to look casual.

MOSEY: (CONT'D) One of life's great mysteries.

JUSTINE: Have you ever tried answering a straight question?

MOSEY: Have you ever tried asking one?

JUSTINE: I just have!

MOSEY: Holy mixed-messages, Batgirl. Are you saying you want me to be in love with you?

JUSTINE: No.

The BOYS chuckle.

JUSTINE: What? No!

JACK: She wants you to fancy her, mate. (*To JUSTINE*) You do.

RYOKO: He's right, you do, you know.

JUSTINE: I don't!

JACK: Not even a little bit...?

JUSTINE: Maybe a bit.

MOSEY: Of course I fancy you.

JUSTINE: Oh. Okay. Course you do. ...Why?

BOYS groan.

HAMZA: Here we go...

JUSTINE: Because I'm...?

MOSEY: Pretty?

JUSTINE: No!

MOSEY: You're better than pretty, J.

JUSTINE: Piss off. Pretty is bullshit. (*beat...*) ...What's better than pretty?

MOSEY: Beautiful.

A moment.

JUSTINE: You are a first class bull-shitter.

MOSEY: That's the problem with the truth. It's just more bullshit, but with facts.

JUSTINE: Okay, got it. We got it. We get it. You've scored your sandwiches, Mosey, you can stop now.

MOSEY: I told you shovel-loads of times... You're beautiful.

But you wouldn't hear me, like you won't hear me now...
It's not my fault I've got the wrong sort of bullshit, Justine.
(breathes)
I know you're waiting for the handsome hero with the
height and the jaw to make you feel more securely like a
princess, but what happens when even he can't wake you
out of your coma? Some curses can't lifted by a kiss.

JUSTINE: Wow. Doctor Mosey. You're a certified head-
shrinker, too? You really are a catch.

MOSEY: Makes two of us.

MOSEY looks round sees the BOYS waiting...

MOSEY: (CONT'D) Anyway...

JUSTINE: Would you have loved me if I'd let you keep using
me?

MOSEY: Justine...

JUSTINE: Or rather my room? You and all your 'bros'? If I'd let
you all move in permanently?

MOSEY: We never asked for that.

JUSTINE: I let you stay all winter. Nearly got evicted twice.

MOSEY: Justine we've been through this...

JUSTINE: Boys all over the floor, using up the hot water and
toilet paper, practically pissing on the chair legs and spray-
ing the place with testosterone. I worked so hard to get that

17

room.

MOSEY: I know.

JUSTINE: We said it was just 'til spring.

MOSEY: And we left the day the clocks changed. A deal's a deal.

JUSTINE: And I never saw you again.

MOSEY: They're my mates. I couldn't just desert them.

JUSTINE: So I deserted you? All of you?

MOSEY: We'd outstayed our welcome. We knew that. And we're grateful.

JUSTINE: You didn't even pretend to want to stay.

MOSEY: I thought I was doing you a favour. I thought I was getting out of your way. You didn't love me, Justine.

JUSTINE: Always an answer for everything. Dick.

MOSEY kisses JUSTINE on the cheek. JUSTINE feels her cheek.

JUSTINE: (CONT'D) Yep. Still cursed.

JUSTINE thrusts a sandwich at MOSEY.

MOSEY: Ta, babe.

JUSTINE: Drop dead.

She hands out sandwiches to HAMZA, JACK and RYOKO.

HAMZA: Thanks Just.

JUSTINE: Shut up.

JACK: Thanks, babe.

JUSTINE: Whatever.

RYOKO: You're a diamond.

JUSTINE: Get a job.

JUSTINE goes back to making sandwiches...

JACK: Guess where we're not staying this winter?

HAMZA: Ah, she'll come round. Just playing hard to get.

RYOKO looks at MOSEY.

RYOKO: You alright, mate?

MOSEY: I'm cool, mate.

RYOKO: Girls are proper long, man.

HAMZA: You know what I mean? 'Get a job.' They are a job.

MOSEY: I need a day off.

JACK: Sod it, let's take a week off.

HAMZA: Make that a couple of months, bruv.

RYOKO: Just enjoy the summer...

MOSEY: Let's just... Breathe.

They inhale the summer air.

MOSEY: (CONT'D) And be Carefree Dudes.

As they raise their sandwiches to their lips. JUSTINE slams down a jar of sugar-free crunchy peanut butter.

JUSTINE: Is that how you do it? Hi-five your bros and crack open a beer and poof, hey presto, you're a squad of carefree dudes? Is that all it takes to be heartlessly brainlessly blissful? A shot of testosterone and a world without women? Actually, ooops, sorry. It's 'girls' isn't it? – DON'T you DARE bite that sandwich while I'm talking to you!

BOYS freeze before biting.

JUSTINE: (CONT'D) What would a carefree boy be doing with a woman? Women demand tedious grown-up bullshit like punctuality and consistency and commitment and conversation. Girls are who you go out with when you're flush. Women are who you run home to when you're broke. Girls cheer-lead, women challenge. Girls giggle when they don't get the joke, women stop laughing when they realise they're the punchline – I'M NOT FINISHED!

BOYS hold back from eating.

JUSTINE: (CONT'D) Women are work. Why bother with
women when there are chicks and babes and bitches and
honeys and hoes up for lame banter, filtered selfie sexting
plus Netflix 'n' chill? Why grow up at all or ever? Why
bother with women in a world overflowing with girls?

JACK: Why bother with boys?

MOSEY: Jack...

JACK: No seriously, if boys are so bad why are you wasting
your superior intellectual breath getting militant with a
stinky sweaty litter of dim-witted pups? Could it be that
there's something about boys? Something that dies when
men become men and lies dried up and forgotten inside
them? Something impulsive? Something exciting? The
deafening rush of gushing androgens, the fascinating mini-
spectacle of bum-fluff straggling into beardage, the leg-
spread swagger of something swollen downstairs – the hint
of a sexy swinging chandelier in the downstairs hallway and
the sweet n sour aroma of burgeoning musk? Is it the
endless preening narcissism, the arrogant assumption of
immortality? The relentless over-exploitation and short-
sighted destruction of our primary resource: youth and
beauty? Is that what's pushing your buttons, accelerating
you from nought to bitter in zero seconds as you spectate
our happy heartless extended adolescence? Is she screaming inside? That part of you that could only watch from
across the segregated playground, trapped inside that
awkward scared skinny disobedient body and too-big too
thinky too brainy brain? Is she is still protesting the unfair
roll of the dice that sent you straight-to-Jail-do-not-pass-

Girl-do-not-collect-200 pounds? Is that why you sit up in your Tower of Judgement trapped like Rapunzel, looking down on all the empty-headed boys and girls? 'Cause you never got to be either?

MOSEY: Jack, mate...

JACK: Why does every female want to pretend that looks don't matter when it's all they ever bloody think about?

JUSTINE: There's more to being a girl than being pretty. And there's more to being a boy than being a dick.

JACK: Then why did you ask if Mosey thought you were pretty?

JUSTINE: I didn't.

RYOKO: Truesay she didn't – technically.

JACK: Okay, what would you have said if you had actually technically completed the full sentence?

JUSTINE: I don't know.

She looks away. JACK feels a stab of guilt. The boys groan.

HAMZA: Don't fall for it, Jack, mate.

JUSTINE: I'm not crying!

HAMZA: (*to JACK*) Don't do it man, don't say it...

JACK: I'm sorry.

22

HAMZA: Urrrrr! Mate!

JACK: I just... I'm sorry, Justine. Mosey's right. You are more than pretty.

HAMZA: What the bumba is going on? She is proper playing you!

JUSTINE: I'm not crying! I just get teary when I'm passionate.

HAMZA: 'Cause you're a girl! Own it!

JUSTINE: I am not crying!

HAMZA: Good! 'Cause quite frankly, it ain't that deep!

RYOKO: Thank you!

MOSEY: Time out lads!

JACK: Yes please.

HAMZA: Of course girls are more than just pretty.

RYOKO: Most of 'em.

HAMZA: But what's wrong with just being pretty anyway?

RYOKO: You know?

HAMZA: What's wrong with just being pretty or cute or fit? Not everybody's 'more than pretty' like you, Justine. Some girls just don't like books, does that make you better than them?

JUSTINE: You know I'm not saying that.

MOSEY: She's not saying that...

HAMZA: What's wrong with girls crying? Men cry.

RYOKO: You cry?

HAMZA: All the time! All the time mate! At least once a year – Cup finals!

Various reactions.

HAMZA: (CONT'D) When your team loses on penalties. Talking to counsellors. Movies where dogs die. Or save people. Any movie with dogs, basically. Tupac singing 'Hey Mama'. When your dad says well done son. Men cry. We just don't cry when we're trying to win an argument. I know, I'm being a dick.

RYOKO: Proper being a dick!

HAMZA: Well, what's wrong with being a dick?

RYOKO: I like dicks!

HAMZA: Some girls like dicks!

RYOKO: I don't mean like that, though.

HAMZA: Some girls like guys who are dicks!

RYOKO: Nothing wrong with being gay or anything...

HAMZA: And some guys like girls who act like chicks. Even when they bomb you with the tear gas.

JACK: Hamza, you need to calm down, mate.

MOSEY: All she's saying is...

HAMZA: Don't mansplain me, bruv. Women can talk for themselves, innit?

JUSTINE: Go suck yourself.

HAMZA: Or maybe not.

JACK: You've made your point, fella.

MOSEY: Just leave her alone, alright?

HAMZA: Real talk, yeah? Some dudes are useless except for when they're standing at attention or trying to make babies – or both – and some girls just want be pretty. And some women just want to be girls and some boys want to be boys who like girls, thick, skinny, tall, short, smart, dozy, young or old. And you may not like it, but that ain't a crime. That's nature. But you wanna drag it out into a pointless militant conflict. And that is because – like all women – you are long. Long – drawn out – endlessly argumentative gotta talk about everything 'til the man caves in and agrees just so he can digest his dinner and get some damn peace long. Now can I eat my damn sandwich? I'm hungry!

And, just as they are about to take a simultaneous bite, SUMMER comes whirling across the stage like a beautiful top. Skirt flying up. THE BOYS stare open-mouthed.

25

IT'S NIGHT AGAIN, the MOON is out and laughing like SUMMER. HAMZA is staring at SUMMER, transfixed.

HAMZA: (CONT'D) Oh, crap.

BACK TO SUNSHINE. Enter JOAN with a camera. Taking photos, firing instructions as SUMMER hits pose after pose.

JOAN: Tina Turner! Barbra Streisand! Madonna! Kylie! Beyoncé! Rihanna! Audrey Hepburn! Kate Moss! Naomi! Tyra! Lupita! Diana! Marilyn, Marilyn, Marilyn! Marilyn! Yesssss! Bette Davis!

SUMMER looks uncertain. Tries something vaguely glamorous.

JOAN: (CONT'D) Bette Davis!

SUMMER tries something equally generic.

JOAN: (CONT'D) Bette! Davis! Girl, what in hell are you doing?

SUMMER: (*Filipino*) I am trying to fake it. But it's not working. I'm sorry. Who is Bette Davis please?

JOAN: (*Deep breath, pinching the bridge of her nose*) Okay, she's young. Young is not a crime, do not hurt her.

SUMMER: Is she a model, please? Or is she an actress?

JOAN: Child. She is everything. Every woman. At our bitchiest and our butchest, our most vengeful and most forgiving, our most beautiful and most grotesque, our most empowering and most terrifying. She is all the sin-inspiring sensuality and uppity intellectual curiosity of Eve and the unapologetic ball-busting inconsistency of nature. She was Meryl before Meryl dreamed of Meryl, she was and is Amelia Earhart, Emily Pankhurst, Florence Nightingale, Harriet Tubman, Marsha P Johnson, Elizabeth the Virgin Queen, Boudicca and all of the Brontës, she is Khadija the first Muslim, She is Kali and all ten gleaming knives, she is Jezebel, Delilah, Mary Magdalene and Mary of Nazareth mother of God... All in one lift of the head...

She lifts her head. SUMMER copies.

JOAN: (CONT'D) ...and a casual exhalation...

JOAN places her vape between SUMMER'S lips.

JOAN (CONT'D) ...of scandalous, shameless... sensual... smoke.

SUMMER vapes, exhales.

JOAN: (CONT'D) And now she is you. You are every woman. Your femininity is your weapon. And every Kingdom is your conquered Queendom. All you have to do is...

SUMMER smiles.

JOAN: (CONT'D, *with quiet intensity*) Yes. That's it. You're ready. Fly baby... Fly...

SUMMER walks smiling, full of sensual carefree confidence past the gaping faces of the BOYS and then she is gone. They stare. They run after SUMMER. Last to go is MOSEY, who looks back at JUSTINE and mouths 'Sorry' as he goes.

JUSTINE: You forgot Joan of Arc.

JOAN: (*Small smile*) No I didn't.

JUSTINE: So you're a... fashion photographer...?

JOAN: No.

JUSTINE: ...Some sort of model booker or scout...?

JOAN: Sorry, I didn't catch your name?

JUSTINE: A madam?

JOAN: Excuse me?

JUSTINE: No judgement!

JOAN: I help certain kinds of women find their confidence.

JUSTINE: 'Certain kinds' of women?

JOAN: Certain kinds, yes.

JUSTINE: Aren't there magazines for that?

JOAN: Not yet. But give me time.

JUSTINE: So, what are your qualifications?

JOAN: I was once myself a certain kind of woman.

JUSTINE: Which kind was that?

JOAN: The uncertain kind. (*offering card*) My card?

JUSTINE: Oh. Cool. (*takes it*) Mine's in my evening bag.
  (*reads*) Your name's Joan?

JOAN: Joan Dark.

JUSTINE: Piss off!

JOAN: Okay.

  JOAN starts to depart.

JUSTINE: Isn't finishing school a bit... old school? Do your
  ladies have to balance books on their heads while getting
  out of sports cars in short skirts without showing their
  knickers? I bet you charge a fortune.

JOAN: Well, that depends.

JUSTINE: I wasn't asking for me. I'm not that kind of girl.
  Woman. Whirl. Lady. I'm not a really a lady-type girl-woman
  -whirl and I think lady-training wouldn't be right for the kind
  of person I want to be. Or am.

JOAN: And what kind of person is that?

  *SUMMER re-enters, is practising the art of spinning so her
  skirt flies up and sitting down before it falls, so that it
  surrounds her perfectly on the grass. Improving rapidly, she
  is impressively, oppressively ladylike. Suddenly JACK appears
  beside her.*

JACK: Alright there, sweetheart?

RYOKO appears.

RYOKO: Oh my *days*, man!

HAMZA appears.

HAMZA: *Baaaaabeee! Baby Baby Baaaaaaaaaby!*

MOSEY appears.

MOSEY: Boo!

SUMMER pulls out a spray can and expertly zaps all four BOYS square in the face.

MOSEY: (CONT'D) AHHHHH!

RYOKO: Shit!

HAMZA: Whoaaahh!

JACK: Jesus Christ, woman!

SUMMER: I'm sorry! I'm sorry, it was a reflex!

JACK: Jesus Christ woman, are you insane?

SUMMER: (*reaching out*) Are you okay?

HAMZA: Don't come near me, you militant man-hating psycho!

MOSEY: Bloody feminists, man!

RYOKO: Mummy!

JOAN: Oh for crying out loud..!

She grabs the spray from SUMMER and sprays all four boys again, full force. They wail louder, then realise they're fine. They open their eyes.

JOAN: (CONT'D) It's Evian spray.

HAMZA: Yeah, but that nut-job blatantly thought it was mace.

JOAN: Yeah, she's real pit-bull this one.

SUMMER smiles a radiantly sweet sorry.

JOAN: (CONT'D) A regular little gangsta bitch.

JOAN beckons the BOYS aside.

JOAN: (CONT'D) But she's cute, right? For such a ball-buster?

They look across at SUMMER. She is playing with her hair.

HAMZA: She's ai'ite.

JOAN: A freshie straight off the plane from the South Seas...
(*calls to SUMMER*) Where you from again, baby?

SUMMER: I am from the Philippines.

JOAN: (*to BOYS*) I mean that's practically Hawaii, right? So
she's a little freaked out by all this first world stuff. Little girl
in the big bad city, you know? She's just sooo obviously

deliciously corruptible, she's pretty much a dog-magnet. What she really needs is someone to look after her a little and show her the real London just for a few hours, you know? So, my plan is to set my girl up on a series of dates over the next few days. Do I... have any volunteers?

Mesmerized, the boys start to slowly raise their hands, then...

HAMZA: Hold up...

The hands stop.

HAMZA: (CONT'D) Can we have a second?

JOAN: Honey, have two, I'm feeling generous.

JOAN moves to one side...

HAMZA: Sorry, but this is weird.

RYOKO: So? We're weird!

JACK: And she's gorgeous.

HAMZA: Exactly.

JACK: Exactly, result!

MOSEY: Hamza's got a point. That babe could get any date she wants. Why would she date a homeless bloke?

RYOKO: She's doesn't know we're homeless, though, does she?

JACK: Maybe she likes one of us and she secretly wants a closer look.

HAMZA: And maybe it's all a big wind-up.

JACK: Maybe she might really fall for one of us and give us all somewhere to crash this winter?

HAMZA: And maybe we all saw how that went last time.

MOSEY: Oh, sorry, four months of sandwiches and central heating weren't good enough?

HAMZA: You know what I mean.

JACK: Well, I don't know about you lot, but I'm going for it.

MOSEY: It's not like we've got anything better on the schedule.

RYOKO: It might be a laugh.
And she is gorgeous.

MOSEY: One for all.

ALL FOUR LADS: And all for fun!

JUSTINE watches SUMMER in appalled awe.

HAMZA: Okay, sod it.

JUSTINE: How long can you do that for? Just play with your hair, like it's the most important thing in the world.

SUMMER: My mother taught me that everything you do is the most important thing in the world, until it's finished. It's done. (*reaching for JUSTINE'S hair*) Would you like to me to...?

JUSTINE: I'm fine.

SUMMER starts to work on JUSTINE'S hair.

SUMMER: Making things better doesn't mean they weren't perfect before.

JUSTINE: I just hate playing with my... It's just hair, right?

SUMMER: Hair is a billboard. You have to be sure your message is clear.

JUSTINE: Sod it.

JUSTINE tries to relax. Watches JOAN negotiate.

JUSTINE: (CONT'D) You do realise she's totally pimping you out, right?

SUMMER: Me? Or them?

JOAN and the BOYS approach SUMMER.

JOAN: Summer, Darling...

JUSTINE: (*sighs*) And your name's Summer... Of course it is.

JOAN: Meet Ryoko, Hamza, Mosey and Jack.

SUMMER: Hello!

The BOYs grunt unspecific noises in return.

SUMMER: (CONT'D) Sorry I maced you with Evian spray.

JOAN: Oh, such a big-hearted girl. Funnily enough, though, it was they who are hoping to apologise to you for leaping outta the long grass at you like lecherous commandos. I told 'em you'd've already forgotten it as you're far too well-raised to hold a grudge, but it seems they insist that each of them would like to take a turn at taking you out.

SUMMER: On a date?

JOAN: Four dates to be precise. Four days, four dates. Don't say mama never hooked you up. And the first one's today.

SUMMER: Today? But my hair needs two days to prepare.

JOAN: Then we better get started now. (*to BOYS*) You cowboys can gallop home and wet-wipe your pits and cologne your scrotums or whatever menfolk do... and Summer will meet whichever lucky dude that draws the long straw back here at shall we say five?

The BOYS exchange looks.

JOAN: (CONT'D) Presume you all reside in the vicinity?

The boys nod and shrug vague yeses.

JOAN: (CONT'D) Then five it is and here it is. (*to JUSTINE*) Five thirty, same spot?

JUSTINE: How much do you charge again?

JOAN: How much can you afford?

JUSTINE: If I can pay you in sandwiches, then prepare to get rich.

JOAN: I was born rich. I'm a woman.

JOAN exits.

SUMMER: I will see one of you at five o'clock?

BOYS smile with nervous bravado.

SUMMER: (CONT'D) Beautiful. I love surprises.

SUMMER starts to leave. JUSTINE reaches up to feel her new hairdo.

SUMMER: (CONTD) (*Dictatorial*) Don't touch it! (*smile*) You're perfect.

SUMMER leaves.

JACK: What the hell just happened?

HAMZA: Have we just been mugged off?

MOSEY: All four of us.

RYOKO: Yup.

JUSTINE: Make that five.

Beat.

RYOKO: I'm excited.

SNAP TO:

FIVE O'CLOCK – OLYMPIC PARK

THE BOYS are getting RYOKO dressed and ready.

RYOKO: (CONT'D) What the bloodclaart am I doing?

MOSEY: You're going on a date, bruv!

RYOKO: Why me?

MOSEY: Why not you?

JACK: You know you're proper slick with the lasses.

RYOKO: That's all front, though! They never actually go for it.
What if she wants me to buy her something? Girls expect
that, don't they?

MOSEY: Some girls.

RYOKO: Well, we know this one does. Look at her. Oh, man I
stink like a skipful of cow-guts.

JACK: Mate, you'll be fine. Just keep her away from your
sweaty bits and remember what your nan said on your first
day of school. 'Just be yourself, love.'

RYOKO: The day I decided to be myself, my nan kicked me

out.

JACK: Well, somebody's nan musta said it! Why're you being so obstructive?

RYOKO: I'm being myself innit? Face it, I'm blatantly gonna screw this up.

JACK: Well don't. You'll screw it up for the rest of us.

RYOKO: What's this?

MOSEY is placing a small bag on RYOKO'S back.

MOSEY: Chillax, bredren. It's the kite.

JACK/HAMZA: Kite?

RYOKO: We were saving that.

MOSEY: Yep. For a special occasion.

RYOKO: What've I told you about saying 'bredren'? Anyone even know how to assemble this thing?

Silence.

RYOKO: (CONT'D) Great. Maybe she won't even turn up. I mean, why should she? She's probably been approached by men with money and a motor and a home.

MOSEY: We've got a home. We just haven't got a roof.

RYOKO: (*grins*) We've got a roof. It just lets in the rain,

38

sometimes.

MOSEY: And a carpet.

RYOKO: Just no walls.

MOSEY: And who needs walls?

JACK: Rehearsal!

MOSEY darts about picking flowers.

RYOKO: You what?

JACK: You heard. You're stood waiting.

RYOKO: Where?

JACK: Right there, waiting.

RYOKO: How long have I been waiting?

JACK: Twenty minutes?

RYOKO: Bitch!

JACK: Cut!

HAMZA: Girls don't like that, fam.

RYOKO: I ain't gonna say it to her face.

JACK: Don't even think it, mate.

HAMZA: Girls read minds.

JACK: Well, moods... girls read moods. So don't be moody or she'll scarper.

HAMZA: And if she vexes you, don't get vexed.

RYOKO: How do I not get vexed if she's vexing me?

JACK/HAMZA: You suck it up, bruv.

HAMZA: Women like to test mans. Just remember – whatever way she finds to wind you up. Stay breezy.

RYOKO: Breezy.

HAMZA: Breezy.

JACK: Take two! You're waiting...

HAMZA: ...Right there...

MOSEY: Wiiiiiith...

MOSEY thrusts a bunch of flowers into RYOKO's grip.

RYOKO: Aren't these a bit corny?

MOSEY: Girls like corny.

HAMZA: They love it, bruv.

MOSEY: At least you look like you're trying.

JACK: And now you've been waiting all breezy with your corny bunch of freshly-nicked flowers...

MOSEY: ...and she turns up at sunset looking like a sunrise...

JACK: ...and you gaze at her bewitched and you say...

RYOKO: (*staring into the distance*) ...You're early.

HAMZA/JACK: Yeaaaahhhhh!!!

HAMZA: Yes, yes, yes, fam! That is the <u>line</u>! I need to write that down!

JACK: Y'see? You're a natural!

MOSEY: Where did that come from?

RYOKO: The sunrise.

He is staring at SUMMER as she enters, looking stunning.

RYOKO: (CONT'D) Hi Summer.

BOYS: (*a bit thrown*) Hi/Hey/Whassup? (*or whatever*)

SUMMER: I hope I'm not late.

RYOKO: I couldn't care less.

RYOKO holds out the flowers as the BOYS position themselves behind SUMMER, so they can signal to RYOKO.

SUMMER: For me?

RYOKO: Actually, no.

BOYS: (*whisper*) 'No'???

RYOKO: I was just giving them a good look at you.

BOYS: (*impressed*) Ohhhhhh...!

RYOKO: (*to the bunch of flowers*) Eat your hearts out, kids.

SUMMER: (*laughing, grabs bouquet*) Oh! (*talks to bouquet*) Don't listen to him! (*cradling them*) Poor children!

RYOKO: Poor everyone. But you've no idea, have you? What it's like for the rest of the world.

MOSEY: Uh-oh!

JACK: Where's this going...?

RYOKO: Having to see ourselves in a mirror after looking at you.

SUMMER: I bet you say that to all the girls.

RYOKO: Only this time it's true.

BOYS: Yesssssss!

MOSEY: Get in!

RYOKO: A bit corny?

SUMMER: Very. Keep going.

BOYS: (*Mouthing*) Keep going!!!

RYOKO: Okay! (*breathes*) So...

SUMMER: So.

RYOKO: My London.

SUMMER: I am in your hands.

RYOKO: You're my bouquet!

MOSEY: This boy's got some skills!

RYOKO: Maybe one day I'll take you up the aisle!

BOYS: (*mouthing in horror*) Noooo!

RYOKO: Nooooo! I mean, walk you down the aisle.

SUMMER: You are such the romantic.

RYOKO: I know, right? I'm proper chirpsing!

SUMMER: Please, what is chirpsing?

RYOKO: It's like birds – singing to each other in the spring.

SUMMER: Ohhh! Yes. You are an excellent chirpsinger.
   (*seeing RYOKO'S smile*) Sorry, my English.

RYOKO: Trust me, it's better than mine.

SUMMER: Well, I am sure your London is better than mine.

RYOKO: I guess we'll see. How far can you walk in those shoes?

SUMMER: These are my walking heels.

RYOKO: I love a practical woman.

RYOKO and SUMMER exit. The BOYS watch them go.

JACK: (*wiping away a mock tear*) Our little baby's all grown up!

MOSEY: He's gonna be fine.

HAMZA: Yep. He's got this. It's not like he needs us to keep an eye on him...

The BOYS are already following RYOKO and SUMMER.

HAMZA: (CONT'D) ...or nothing.

THE BOYS exit. JUSTINE and JOAN arrive.

JUSTINE: I wore my best dress.

JOAN: Right.

JUSTINE: Where's your camera?

JOAN: That's not a first session thing. The camera can wait.

JUSTINE: For a better dress?

JOAN: This isn't about a dress. This is about what's in the

dress.

JUSTINE: You sure? I've been practising my twirl, see?

JUSTINE spins her dress. It flares up. Someone whistles.

JUSTINE: (CONT'D) Fuck off! (*To JOAN*) Sorry. (*To the whistler*) Sorry.

JOAN: Why are you saying sorry?

JUSTINE: To you or him?

JOAN: To anyone.

JUSTINE: Well, I'm saying sorry to him because he can't help being a Neanderthal ninny with maximum entitlement and zero manners who's a victim of a lifetime of intense cultural programming and peer pressure, and telling him to fuck off is like commanding a child with Tourette's to stop swearing or a brutalized dog to stop pissing on the floor.

JOAN: Okay.

JUSTINE: And I'm saying sorry to you for wasting your time.

JOAN: Is that the plan?

JUSTINE: It's what I do. I waste time. I wasted an entire childhood pretending to be someone else. I wasted more time struggling to explain to everyone around me who I really was and how I felt, when all I actually know is how I don't feel and who I'm not. I'm standing there in front of my father and mother and the look of confusion on their faces

45

is identical. She doesn't recognize me any more than he does. She doesn't know this girl. This woman. This daughter that she never painted the nursery for. All she sees is failure. All those years of investment, of attempts at affection, of ignoring strangeness and hoping it will go away, all wasted. On a kid that dismisses the name they thought so hard about and has to practise twirling (*twirling*) a thousand fucking times – (*someone WHISTLES*) Fuck off! – just to learn how to stop falling over. All that love wasted on someone who doesn't know how to take a compliment. For years I've been watching girls get whistled at by gangs and secretly wishing I could be the one yelling fuck off. How screwed up is that?

JOAN: About average. Where are you going?

JUSTINE is leaving.

JUSTINE: Home! To put on some comfortable footwear! Not everyone can stilt-walk like Naomi Campbell.

JOAN: Is this how you dealt with mommy and daddy? By walking away?

JUSTINE: Excuse me? Fuck you!

JOAN: No, excuse me and fuck you, princess! You think you're the only woman alive who disappointed her mother? The only one in the world who's struggling with identifying a genuine compliment and knowing how to spot a glass ceiling disguised as a pretty mirror? You think you're the one lonely soul in the world who's confused? That's part of the job description. You'll see it listed in the Human Section under Required Skills – 'Must be willing to work shit out.'

Now, you can go home to practise falling over on your twirls and feeling sorry for yourself, or we can stay right here on this hot-as-hell day and work this shit out. Either way you owe me a sandwich, girl, 'cause my time is money and you promised me bread.

JOAN holds out a hand. JUSTINE gives her a sandwich.

JOAN: (CONT'D) Thank you.

JUSTINE: It's vegan soul-food.

JOAN: Soul-food, huh? ...Great. First lesson. After me... 'I...'

JUSTINE: I.

JOAN: '...am...'

JUSTINE: Am.

JOAN: '...my own.'

JUSTINE: My own.

JOAN: Put it together.

JUSTINE: I.... Am... My Own.

JOAN nods commandingly.

JUSTINE: (CONT'D) I am my own.

JOAN nods.

JUSTINE: (CONT'D) I am my own. I am my own... I am my own what?

JOAN: We'll see. Back here, right here, 8 pm sharp. No make-up, no heels and your plainest dress. Meanwhile, repeat the mantra. If you don't I'll know.

JUSTINE: Wow, you are tough.

JOAN: (*smiles*) Isn't it great?

THREE HOURS LATER

PRIMROSE HILL/OLYMPIC PARK

SUMMER and RYOKO are walking up the hill. He is holding his shoes in his hand. She is still wearing her heels.

RYOKO: Wow you are tough!

SUMMER: I simply love walking, that's all.

RYOKO: That was 11 miles though. In kilometres that's... like...

SUMMER: Seventeen kilometres.

RYOKO: Seventeen!

SUMMER: Point seven.

RYOKO: To be exact. Don't look round! You promised. You probably had to walk that far every day, though, yeah? Growing up.

SUMMER: Good guess.

RYOKO: To fetch clean water from a well.

SUMMER: To get to school.

RYOKO: Rah. My school was at the end of the street and I only went there twice a year. First day and last.

SUMMER: You didn't like education?

RYOKO: You'd never guess, I know, I'm so blatantly a brain-box. So why did you come here, then? Sorry, stupid question – Don't look yet! – I used to ask my grandma and grandad that too. 'Why did you come here? All the way from the land of the banana tree, to this rainy little cloud off the coast of Europe?'

SUMMER: What did they answer?

RYOKO: 'So you could be somebody.' Turned out I was the wrong somebody.

SUMMER: Where were they from?

RYOKO: Some other small island.

SUMMER: Ah small islands... Good to grow up on. But better to grow out of.

RYOKO: Britain is an island too, though.

SUMMER: Yes, but somehow here it is easier not to notice.

RYOKO: Bigger country, more people yeah?

SUMMER: There are more that 100 million people in the Phillipines.

RYOKO: Rah.

SUMMER: On 7,175 islands.

RYOKO: Rah. Still, I guess the world's just a bunch of small islands? And some people never outgrow 'em. Sod this. Forget about them. They had their chance.

SUMMER: You don't talk to your grandparents?

RYOKO: I've given up trying.

SUMMER: They threw you out?

RYOKO: They froze me out. So I never went back. I outgrew their island.

They arrive at the summit.

RYOKO: (CONT'D) We reached!

SUMMER: I can turn around?

RYOKO: Only if you want to.

SUMMER: What if I don't like what I see?

RYOKO: What do you mean?

SUMMER: Will you want to forget me?

RYOKO: Wait! Are you putting all this on me? (*deep breath*) Breezy.... (*forced breezy*) Ah, you know families are like... When was the last time you spoke to yours?

SUMMER: Today.

RYOKO: Well that's lovely. Cool.

SUMMER: Five minutes ago.

RYOKO: You what?

SUMMER: Now. I'm speaking to them now. Everything I do, everything I see, I share with them.

RYOKO: Oh my God, why have the pretty ones always got a screw loose?

SUMMER: Just because they don't know how to speak to me yet, I don't need to forget how to speak to them. It took me a long time to accept myself, it will take them a while too.

RYOKO: You know what, Oprah? That's bollocks.

SUMMER: Excuse me, what is bollocks, please?

RYOKO: Shit. That's all bullshit. It's utter total unvarnished crap. I accepted them, with all their hypocrisy and fake religiousness, pretending to love Jesus when they hate everything he preached and stood for. I accepted when they told me violence was a kindness. I accepted and accepted, until one day I realised I ain't Jesus, and I don't have to die for no one else's sins. And I ain't gonna die for theirs, you get me? And I don't have to think about what they think or about what they want or whether they're alive or dead. I don't have to think about them, full stop. Period. Breezy.

SUMMER: And this is working?

RYOKO: Eh?

SUMMER: You have stopped thinking about them?

RYOKO: Oh my dayyyys! This is blatantly the worst date ever!!! I've dragged our sweaty arses all across the smoggy city and up a bloody mountain and now you're giving me a stress episode and you won't even look round at the view.

SUMMER: (*Looking at RYOKO*) I am looking at the view right now.

RYOKO: Okay. Let's reboot this. I'm breezy. I'm breezy and I'm sorry.

SUMMER: Yes.

RYOKO: I'm really sorry.

SUMMER: Yes.

RYOKO: And how about you?

SUMMER: I'm very good thank you. What is breezy, please?

RYOKO: Cool. Relaxed.

SUMMER: You are not breezy.

RYOKO: I'm trying.

SUMMER: Yes.

RYOKO: Soo... Isn't it your turn to say sorry?

SUMME: For what am I sorry?

RYOKO: I said sorry to you!

SUMMER: For what?

RYOKO: For being an idiot.

SUMMER: I am not an idiot.

RYOKO: Who the hell have you come as? Dr Spock? You don't have to only state facts, you know. Sorry's not a confession or nothing. Sometimes people just say it to make each other feel better. Like, 'Sorry that I hurt your feelings.'

SUMMER: But I didn't hurt your feelings. They were already hurt.

RYOKO: Oh my DAYYYS!!! What is your bumbaclaart raasclaart issue??

THE BOYS come running up the hill.

MOSEY: Bruuuuv! Bruv Bruv Bruv!

JACK: Okay, time out!!

RYOKO: What the fuck are you? A fembot?

HAMZA: (*to SUMMER*) Just give us a second will you, please? Fam, you blatantly need to take a chill pill and sit yourself down on Chill Hill, yeah?

MOSEY runs in with his hood up and a handful ice lollies.

MOSEY: Ice lollies!!

JACK: That's my boyyyy!

JACK grabs the ice-cream, while MOSEY swiftly removes and hides his hoody.

JACK: (CONT'D) (*to SUMMER*) Hey darlin', how about we have a little visit together while our brothers have a quick impromptu business chat, yeah? Yeah, darlin'? Can you take one of these nice cool lifesavers off my hands?

MOSEY and JACK sit. JACK holds up a lolly. SUMMER takes it.

SUMMER: Thank you.

She sits. Her back to the view.

RYOKO: (*struggling for composure*) That trainer bird has turned this poor girl into a flippin' fembot, bruv! She's got no discernible feelings. I'm done here. No one's that pretty.

HAMZA: Someone is.

Beat.

HAMZA: (CONT'D) Someone somewhere is pretty enough to go through all this insanity for. And there will be insanity, man. And you're gonna need coping skills. What better training than with a fembot?

RYOKO: You know what I'm like, man. My buttons get pushed proper easy.

HAMZA: What was she saying?

RYOKO: Just stuff about stuff. My situation. She doesn't get it. She stands there immovable. Then she starts digging at me. Trying to get me to face things.

HAMZA: You know women chat shit. Just let 'em talk and stand aloof, yeah?

RYOKO: What if they insist on telling the truth, though?

HAMZA: I dunno. Maybe fight fire with fire and come back with truth? Okay, I know most things ain't that simple. But this one might be. Maybe – way back in the day, before she lost the plot with you – grandma was right?

RYOKO makes his way over to SUMMER.

RYOKO: I do miss them. I do wonder how they are, if they're alive and if they think about me and the things they said. Whether they've searched the bible to see if they can find me. But I don't want to miss them. I don't want to wonder about them. Because I know that if I was moved to see them again, I'd only hurt myself. Like I used to. I know it's not their fault. They're just the trigger not the whole gun. I know there's probably a right way to handle 'em. But today

I don't want to handle 'em. I want to be in the sun with someone beautiful, and I want to show her a view of my city and try to fly this poxy kite that I don't know how to build on a mad humid day with no breeze. But I stick to what I'm skilled at and flip out. That's me. But I don't want to be that me. I want to be the other happy me that's good at chirpsing and dates and maybe cops a little cuddle in the grass on a summer afternoon. Can you help me with that? You don't have to marry me. But can you help?

SUMMER: Kite please.

RYOKO pulls the kite from his back and hands it to SUMMER, who hands MOSEY her lolly as she starts to assemble it. RYOKO looks on amazed. The other BOYS lay back and lick their lollies at the sky, MOSEY enjoying two.

JUSTINE returns in simpler dress. Very little make-up.

She twirls. Someone whistles.

JUSTINE: Oh, come on! Are you kidding me?

JOAN: You don't think you deserved that?

JUSTINE: You're joking right? In this?

JOAN: It's not about the –

JOAN/JUSTINE: – dress –

JUSTINE: (*overlapping*) – it's about what's in the dress. This is not a feminist workshop, Justine, bitch, get over it. Oh, God, there's that face.

JOAN: Is a woman who likes being whistled at a bad feminist?

JUSTINE: Well, she's hardly radical.

JOAN: Is there a radical etiquette book? How liberating. Are you a bad feminist, Justine? Are you a bad woman?

JUSTINE: (*quietly*) Maybe... I don't know.

JOAN: What do you know?

JUSTINE: (*very quietly*) I am my own.

JOAN: What was that?

JUSTINE: I am my own.

JOAN: You are your what?

JUSTINE: I am my own.

JOAN: Yes, you are. Now, did you happen to bring another soul-food sandwich?

JUSTINE produces a sandwich.

JOAN: (CONT'D) Perfect. Let's picnic.

JOAN nestles into the grass, the perfect lady. JUSTINE settles down to face her, adjusting repeatedly, trying to copy. JOAN takes a flask from her bag, unscrews the top, pours a drink into the lid-cup, pinkie up, and sips. JUSTINE studies JOAN'S hands. JOAN hands the flask and cup to JUSTINE, who tries to copy every gesture. JOAN unwraps the sandwich and takes a bite.

JOAN: (CONT'D) (*trying to work out what what's she's eating and whether she likes it*) Mmmmmm. What are you doing?

JUSTINE: (*almost spilling*) Mmm?

JOAN: Why are you holding it like that?

JUSTINE: Why were you holding it like that?

JOAN: Because I'm me. You are not me. You are...

JUSTINE: ...My own.

   JUSTINE changes her grip. Changes it again. Again... Again...

JOAN: Goddam it, just hold it!

JUSTINE: I don't know how to hold it!

   JOAN reaches out to steady JUSTINE'S hand...

JOAN: Just hold it like you're gonna drink it. Any way you want. Like nobody's watching.

JUSTINE: Someone's always watching.

JOAN: Then let 'em see you. What do you have to hide?

   JUSTINE drinks.

JOAN: (CONT'D) Okay...

JUSTINE spills a drop.

JUSTINE: Ohhhh! You see?

JOAN: Don't worry about it. Maybe if you sat more comfortably? More like you.

JUSTINE: Trouble is, more like me is more like this.

JUSTINE sits legs open.

JUSTINE: (CONT'D) And when I sit like that, I do this... (*a series of unladylike poses*) ...and this... And this.

JOAN: Girls sit like that.

JUSTINE: But on me it's not very... lady-like.

JOAN: Seems to be like this lady.

JUSTINE: So I should just go galumphing about, like a great gangly rhino?

JOAN: Sorry, are female rhinos not lady rhinos?

JUSTINE: Well...

JOAN: You see a woman on the street. Big boots, big stride, galumphing about. Not feminine enough?

JUSTINE: Um...

JOAN: Big butch dyke? Bit butt. Big boobs. Un-shaved legs. Not a woman?

JUSTINE: Definitely a woman.

JOAN: Now define feminist.

JUSTINE: Person who is committed to the social, financial, political and personal equality of the sexes.

JOAN: Nothing to do with femininity?

JUSTINE: No.

JOAN: Feminists can wear make-up?

JUSTINE: Feminists can wear make-up.

JOAN: Feminists can have moustaches?

JUSTINE: Some women have moustaches. Lots of women.

JOAN: Beautiful women?

JUSTINE: Yes. ...Yes.

JOAN thrusts a wet-wipe at JUSTINE.

JOAN: Wipe.

JUSTINE looks down.

JOAN: (CONT'D) The face. We said no make-up.

JUSTINE: I'm hardly...

JOAN: The lip gloss.

JUSTINE wipes.

RYOKO: Over there.

SUMMER: Where?

RYOKO points.

RYOKO: That tall grey place on the horizon. 20th floor.

SUMMER: That one all on its own like the cactus? It's beautiful.

RYOKO: From here, maybe.

SUMMER: Are there windows on this side? Can they see us?

RYOKO: On days like this they can maybe see the kites. Shame there's no breeze...

Cue the BREEZE that snatches the kite from SUMMER's hands, RYOKO runs after it and catches its string... It lifts.

RYOKO: (CONT'D) Rah. Where'd that come from?

JOAN: Lie back.

JUSTINE looks at her.

JOAN: (CONT'D) Don't think about it.

JOAN lies back.

JOAN: (CONT'D) Just lie back.

SUMMER holds the kite with RYOKO. They fly it together.

JOAN: (CONT'D) Anyway you want to. Let your skirt do its thing, yes, kick off your shoes, feel the grass on your body and the sun on your skin and take a break from giving a damn. Breathe out... Breathe in. Are you a gangly rhino now?

JUSTINE: I don't think so. No.

JOAN: And what would a lady do now? To be more of a lady?

JUSTINE: She might cross her legs.

JOAN: Would that make her happier?

JUSTINE: Maybe.

JOAN: Would it make you happier?

SUMMER goes and puts her arm around RYOKO. Alarmed, he looks round at the BOYS. They give him a gleeful thumbs up. RYOKO sniffs under his arm, then slips it around SUMMER. They relax into a cuddle.

JUSTINE makes a tiny sound. JOAN glances at her. JUSTINE is crying. Then weeping.

JOAN reaches out along the grass to take JUSTINE'S hand. JUSTINE sobs at the sky. She subsides a little.

As RYOKO looks out at the view, with the hand that holds

the kite string, RYOKO and SUMMER give the horizon a little wave.

JUSTINE: Thank you.

THE BOYS lift a hand and wave at the horizon too.

SUNSET

THE BOYS all in their sleeping bags.

RYOKO is feverish, thrashing. Talking to himself.

RYOKO: It's wasn't me! ...I wasn't me!

MOSEY: Ryoko...

RYOKO: Don't touch me. ...Don't touch me!

MOSEY touches RYOKO. Who jolts awake.

MOSEY: It's okay! It's me. Come here.

MOSEY uses his shirt to dry RYOKO off.

MOSEY: (CONT'D) You're shivering. Are you cold?

RYOKO: I'm freezing.

MOSEY: You're probably dehydrated. Hang on.

MOSEY fetches some water.

MOSEY: (CONT'D) Used to happen to me on long runs.

RYOKO: You were a runner?

MOSEY: In another life. (*hands over the bottle*) Maybe we should go hospital.

RYOKO: No!

MOSEY: Okay.

RYOKO: Promise me. No hospitals. Ever.

MOSEY: How can I promise that?

RYOKO: Promise.

MOSEY: Promise. Maybe it's a love fever.

RYOKO: Leave it out!

MOSEY: You liked her didn't you? She liked you.

RYOKO: No.

MOSEY: The way she looked at you when you were both holding that kite. You didn't see it?

RYOKO: There was nothing to see. I'm not lovable like that.

MOSEY: Says who?

RYOKO: I'm not eligible. She'll like you though. You'll sweep her right off her Jimmy Choos with your flowers and your gentlemanliness. Is that even a word?

MOSEY: It's definitely a thing. She'll choose you. She's got taste.

They smile. Suddenly MOSEY'S eyes roll back in his head.

RYOKO: Oh, shit... Mosey!

MOSEY falls to the ground in a violent epileptic fit.

RYOKO: (CONT'D) Oh, no! Oh no!

RYOKO tries to give MOSEY water, it goes everywhere. RYOKO holds MOSEY in his arms, riding the storm. They lie together. RYOKO spooning MOSEY as the twitching subsides.

RYOKO: (CONT'D) See that? Shooting star. Some things never get old however many times you see 'em. You see 12 an hour where my grandparents are from. But here you have to keep your eyes open. That's the only thing about summer in London. Light pollution. This is almost nice isn't it? My turn to look after you. Almost kind of lovely. I know I'm being selfish. Forgive me. I hope she chooses you Ry. She will choose you. ...Who wouldn't?

Clouds scud across the moon...

SUMMER MOON smiles... then blows a kiss.

HAMZA wakes with a start. He hisses....

HAMZA: Uhhhh! For crying out loud! Go! Away!

SUNRISE

OLYMPIC PARK

The BOYS are helping JACK get ready for his date. JACK is holding an umbrella.

MOSEY: Just focus on your opening approach, yeah. Romeo Ryoko set the bar pretty high yesterday.

RYOKO and MOSEY high five.

RYOKO: Meaning it's your job to take it to the next level and hold her hand.

HAMZA: Oh my God, her <u>whole</u> hand? You lot are such playas!

RYOKO: And then it's the next dude's mission to go for the kiss.

MOSEY: A kiss?

RYOKO: It's all about levels.

JACK: Like a video game!

HAMZA: How old are we again? You lot are so moist!

MOSEY: Wind your neck in Hamz, it's just banter.

HAMZA: You're giving me nausea, though. Why you gotta act so melt? She's just a human in a skirt.

MOSEY: Dude...

HAMZA: It's not like any of us is getting the chance anytime soon to do much more than sniff Princess Manila. Seeing as nobody here's got a bed.

JACK: What we do have is the most exciting city in the world with a million things to do for free and a heat-wave.

HAMZA: As long as it lasts.

MOSEY: It is still August.

HAMZA: Nearly September.

RYOKO: Could have an Indian Summer.

HAMZA: This is England. It could snow this afternoon.

JACK: Hamza mate, is misery your religion? If you ever stumbled on a good time, you'd run a mile crying your heart out.

HAMZA: It's easy to be romantic for free when you don't need to go indoors.

RYOKO: Hamza! Enough. It's not snowing, and it's not September!

Suddenly, out of nowhere, a leaf falls. The BOYS stare until it gently touches down.

Enter SUMMER. More stunning than ever.

SUMMER: I'm sorry I'm late.

JACK: You're not late... (*grabbing the bouquet MOSEY thrusts at him*) ...I'm lucky.

SUMMER reaches into the bouquet, takes out a flower, puts it in JACK'S buttonhole. JACK melts. Hands SUMMER the bouquet. Pulls a bloom out of it and places it behind SUMMER's ear. Offers her his arm. She takes it. JACK opens the umbrella. It's a parasol. He shades SUMMER as he leads her off past the BOYS. They nod approvingly. Respect. He discreetly punches the air.

JACK: (CONT'D) *Yes!*

The BOYS watch them leave. Then approach a flower bed, pick a bloom each, place them in their lapels and follow.

JUSTINE is by her bicycle, making sandwiches, while JOAN watches sitting on a swing.

JUSTINE: ...juicy sundried tomatoes, pine-nuts... No allergy?

JOAN shakes her head.

JUSTINE: (CONT'D) Four crispy strips of grilled tofu bacon...

JOAN: Bacon?

JUSTINE: Tofu bacon.

JOAN: Mmmmm!

JUSTINE: And we have lift off.

JUSTINE delivers the sandwich to JOAN.

JOAN: So, this is actually –

JUSTINE: – One of my passions? Actually, yeah. Who knew?

JOAN: (*chewing non-committally*) Mmmm. Who knew?

JUSTINE: And there you have it all.

JOAN: Mm?

JUSTINE: The three things I love doing that you asked me to show you. Loving food. Making food. And feeding people.

JOAN: Hell, no! Loving food isn't something you 'do'.

JUSTINE: It's something I do.

JOAN: You knew full well what I meant, missy.

JUSTINE: (*Smiles*) I did, which is why I brought...

Produces a ukelele.

JUSTINE: (CONT'D) This is another three in one: Loves music. (*pings a string*) Can't play music. Loves writing songs. (*starts to strum*) Can't write music. Loves to sing... Can't sing.

JUSTINE sings.

CANAL

A boat floats, JACK is rowing. SUMMER, wearing the

bouquet flowers in her hair, holds a parasol, trails a hand in the water listening to music through headphones.

JACK: (*Only half-joking*) So, do you love me yet? Borrowed you a boat, found you a parasol. What's left except to get married?
(*Immediately carried away*)
Oh, can you imagine it though? We'd live in a barge and our kids would have lifebelt babygrows, they'd be all little and cute and multicultural. Imagine my eyes and your eyes mixed! Even Nigel Farage would melt, if he don't have a heart attack.
I'm proper outdoorsy, me. And I can make things. I could make us a boat and a house. And a houseboat. What do you want? I'll make it for you! I'm making you laugh. That's good, ain't it? Girls like boys that make 'em laugh. Summer, have you ever been in love? Don't answer that. I know I'm being weird. I'm sorry. I'm just... this would be such a great story to tell our grand-kids.

JACK gently lifts one of SUMMER'S headphones.

JACK: (CONT'D) You like the song?

She hands JACK his CLOCK RADIO.

SUMMER: I love the song. Thank you.

JUSTINE'S SONG ends.

JOAN: I thought you couldn't sing?

JUSTINE: So did I.

JOAN: Well, something else we've learned today is that the three-in-one-thing still won't fly. One more thing to show. Something you love to do.

JUSTINE: Well, there's this.

JUSTINE kisses JOAN.

A SECOND BOAT floats into view. RYOKO and MOSEY rowing, HAMZA standing up.

HAMZA: Boat ahoy!

JUSTINE: But it's been a while.

JOAN: Well, you're certainly not out of practise.

RYOKO: I wonder if he's told her he loves her yet?

MOSEY: Isn't that usually your trick, Hamza?

HAMZA: Yeah, but Jack's so dozy, he thinks he means it!

JOAN is coolly fixing her lipstick.

JUSTINE: Sorry.

JOAN: No problem. Well done. Full marks.

JUSTINE: I thought you said it wasn't a test?

JOAN: I guess I was wrong. Who knew?

JUSTINE: And now?

JOAN: I was going to ask you the same thing.

JACK: So which part did you like best?

SUMMER: The words.

JACK: It's an instrumental.

SUMMER: Your words.

JACK: You heard all that I was saying...?

SUMMER: I read your lips. Except the part at the end when you turned away.

JACK: (*glancing to the skies*) Just strike me down now...

THUNDER. ALL look up.

JACK: (CONT'D) Hellfire!

HAMZA: Backside!

JACK: I never meant literally!

The sky darkens.

MOSEY: Where did that come from?

Lightning.

BOYS: Shit!

JUSTINE and JOAN draw closer together as JOAN holds her

bag over their heads. JOAN's body heat takes JUSTINE by surprise. She stares at her, mesmerized. Until JOAN turns and kisses JUSTINE.

SUMMER closes her parasol.

JACK: What you doing, darlin'? That's not metal. Though lighting does strike wood... Would you like my jacket?

SUMMER: It's not going to rain. Not here. See over there? That's a baby summer storm. You can hear it.

The distant sound of RAIN on water.

JACK: Oh, yeah!

BOYS: Oh, yeah!

SUMMER: But here... it's still summer.

She takes JACK's surprised hand. JACK recovers, turns and smiles blissfully at the BOYS. HAMZA and RYOKO give him a grinning thumbs up. MOSEY sighs and looks at the sky.

MOSEY: Still summer.

There is a gust of wind that ripples all their clothes.

Watching the sky, no one sees the small flurry of leaves falling behind them.

INTERVAL

PARTY IN THE PARK – NIGHT TIME

JUSTINE and JOAN look at one another. They look like a hot Saturday night.

JOAN: Wow.

JUSTINE: That's my line.

JOAN: No one's stopping you.

JUSTINE: ...Wow.

Beat. They stare. Then...

JUSTINE: (CONT'D) Okay, before we go further...

JOAN: Okay, call me controlling but...

JOAN/JUSTINE: I just need to check...

JUSTINE: This is a date, isn't it?

JOAN: Well, I hope so.

JUSTINE: I just wanted to be certain that this wasn't one of your workshops. Sorry.

JOAN: Oh, no, God, I totally get it. There's been a couple of occasions when I've realised... I'm on the only one on the date. The other person is just...

JUSTINE: 'Hanging out'?

JOAN: God, I hate hanging out.

JUSTINE: 'We're just hanging out'. No special occasion.

JOAN: No need to get your hair did.

JUSTINE: No need to make any effort.

JOAN: No need to meet my friends.

JUSTINE: No need to make a time or place, just –

JOAN: – keeping it spontaneous –

JUSTINE: – keeping it casual.

JOAN: Keeping it loose.

JUSTINE: I hate casual.

JOAN: I hate loose.

JUSTINE: And chill. But the worst line is 'It's complicated'.

JOAN: Good I hate It's complicated.

JUSTINE: Complicated is stupid.

JOAN: Complicated is ridiculously simplistic. Screw complicated.

JUSTINE: Sod complicated! That's so sweet. We hate all the same things.

JOAN: And we both made an effort.

JUSTINE: Yeah? (*smile*) Yeah.

JOAN: I'd say one of us went all out.

JUSTINE: (*big smile*) Yeah. 'Cause I'm on a date.

JOAN/JUSTINE: We're on a date.

JUSTINE: (*bigger smile*) Yeah.

JOAN: God, this is corny.

JUSTINE: (*huge smile*) Yeah.

From behind their backs, JOAN and JUSTINE produce a single rose. They laugh. They accept them. JOAN holds out a hand. The lights all change.

JUSTINE: (CONT'D) And she holds out her hand. And all of sudden you find yourself thinking in spoken word. 'Her hand her hand, there's a world in her hand.' Soft and strong, open and safe, Venus's half-shell beckoning you to bathe. A gently swaying cradle. A hammock hand, whispering for you to climb in and get yourself some sorely needed sunshine and hard-earned rest. So hard to resist, so impossible to believe. Is it really this simple? This natural? This uncompli-cated? A hand? Is all this in a hand?

JOAN: And then there's the music. Why is there always music? Queer souls, maverick spirits and peoples of colour... How is it that outsiders and the underclass feel compelled to make sounds and shapes to mark moments of intensity?

They enslave us and we sing. They separate us and we beat drums or our chests or thighs, determined to speak to one another through dissident beats that only we hear yet everyone feels. And we dance. They insist on seeking to silence us and we dance louder. They persist in attempting to crush us and we dance harder. In circles or lines, in barns, churches, fields, soul trains, mosh pits, weddings, wakes or rent parties, cheek to cheek or booty to booty, hands in the air or only with our eyes... in plantation chain-gangs or on the streets at Stonewall, we dance.

JUSTINE: And when we see someone lovely our first human impulse is to ask them to dance with us.

JOAN: And on the brave occasions when we dare to hold out our hand...

JUSTINE: ...sometimes someone takes it.

JOAN: And we dance.

JUSTINE: We dance.

JOAN: We dance.

JOAN and JUSTINE dance.

FIREWORKS.

Sound FX – great big Ooooohs from the ravers.

MEANWHILE....

MUFFLED MUSIC.

MOSEY is lost in a forest of silhouettes.

MOSEY: Summer! Summer! Where on Earth??? Summer!

LOUD MUSIC. We see HAMZA, JACK and RYOKO. Jumping up and down to the boom of the bass, lost in it.

MOSEY: (CONT'D) Jack mate!

JACK: Yeah, mate!

MOSEY: You seen Summer?

JACK: She's with Mosey!

MOSEY: Mosey??

JACK: Last time I saw her.

MOSEY: I'm Mosey?

JACK: Are you? Shit! Oh yeah! Then I can't help you, mate!

MOSEY: Thanks mate.

JACK: You've not lost her have you?

MOSEY: (*moving on swiftly*) Course not!

JACK: 'Cause that's my future wife you're looking after!

MOSEY: ...Hamza, man!

HAMZA: Yeah, man!

MOSEY: You seen Summer?

HAMZA: She's with you, innit?

MOSEY: You can see she ain't with me!

HAMZA: Oh yeah! Women! They're proper slippery!

MOSEY: Thanks man!

HAMZA: You ain't lost her have you?

MOSEY: No! ...Ryoko, bruv!

RYOKO: Yeah, bruv! Where's Summer?

MOSEY: I lost her bruv!

RYOKO: You what? Where bruv?

MOSEY: If I knew where she was she wouldn't be lost! She was right there, and then she was....

RYOKO: What?

MOSEY: ...then she wasn't. We was into the music, sky stroking, you know – and she said she wanted a drink and I was looking round –

RYOKO: – For a drink to nick, yeah –

MOSEY: – and when I looked back where she was –

RYOKO: – You'd lost her –

MOSEY: – she weren't there.

RYOKO: ...Hamza!

MOSEY: Don't involve Hamza...

RYOKO: Hamza, man! Jack, mate!

HAMZA: Yeah, man?

JACK: What mate?

RYOKO: He's lost her!

HAMZA: You mean she's lost him.

JACK: What did you say to her, mate?

MOSEY: Nothing!

JACK: Maybe that's the problem!

HAMZA: She'll be back! They all come back!

JACK: You got to talk to them, mate!

HAMZA: She'll be back when she's run out of mugs to buy her drinks!

RYOKO: Have you seen her, though?

HAMZA/JACK: She's with Mosey!

RYOKO: (*to MOSEY*) She's with Mosey, bruv! She's fine!

MOSEY: For crying out... I'm Mosey!

RYOKO: For real? Then who's Summer dancing with?

Sure enough, there's SUMMER, a short distance away. Lost in the music.

MOSEY: Is that Summer?

RYOKO: Well, if that ain't her, it's a heck of a convincing body-snatcher.

JACK: That's her alright. Listen to her body language... 'Jaaaaack! Marry me!'

RYOKO: (*handing MOSEY a drink*) ...here you go.

HAMZA: ...there you go. She won't even notice you've been gone. ...If you ever go back there.

JACK: You alright, mate?

RYOKO: This is your moment, bruv! Look at her! Eyes closed, head back... Just begging for a cheeky peck.

JACK: Steady on.

RYOKO: That's the mission. Cheeky peck.

JACK: That was before she held my hand though and fell madly in love.

RYOKO: It's just a cheeky little peck.

MOSEY: Cheeky little peck.

JACK: On the cheek! That's definitively cheeky!

MOSEY: Cheeky little peck...

MOSEY approaches.

JACK: No tongues!

HAMZA: Why you torturing the boy?

RYOKO: He'll be alright.

MOSEY watches SUMMER, lost in herself.

RYOKO: (CONT'D) Cheeky peck, cheeky peck, cheeky peck...

JACK: On the cheek, on the cheek, on the cheek...

MOSEY u-turns back towards them. The BOYS groan.

HAMZA: Loooooong!

RYOKO: You cool?

MOSEY is knocking back SUMMER'S drink.

MOSEY: Born cool! Beyond cool. Cool. Cool... she just looks so... happy as she was, really. You know what I mean?

RYOKO: Well, yeah...

MOSEY: It just seemed rude to interrupt, really.

MOSEY finishes the drink.

MOSEY: (CONT'D) Have you ever been in that place when you want to just... be?

HAMZA: Fuck sake! What is wrong with you?

JACK: Hamz...

HAMZA: Especially you! Acting like you found wifey! Who the hell even is this bitch?

JACK: Don't call her a bitch, mate.

HAMZA: Seriously who is she? Where is she actually from? What is her surname? What's her story? What's her scheme? What's her angle?

RYOKO: She's from Philippines ain't she?

JACK: Seriously, please do not call her a bitch, mate...

HAMZA: Oh, yeah, Philippines. How many islands was it?

RYOKO: Seven thousand one hundred and seventy-five.

HAMZA: Which one's she from? City or village? House, flat or shack? Rich family or poor family? Is she an asylum seeker or a gold-digger after a green card? I know this much – she ain't a princess, even though she acts like one. She's just some woman on a date! As a flippin' exercise! Why do you all feel the need to be so hung up and such pussy-whipped pussies about her?

MOSEY: What's wrong with pussies?

RYOKO: Actually I quite like pussies.... On the right person.

JACK: Why you being so fanny-phobic, mate?

HAMZA: I've told you about getting deep. Stay focused. This is about the kiss, yeah?

MOSEY: Or maybe it's about you.

HAMZA: 'Scuse me?

MOSEY: You and the way you talk about people.

MOSEY grabs JACK's drink and finishes it.

MOSEY: (CONT'D) Specifically female people.

HAMZA: What the fuck are you –

MOSEY: Surprise, dude! Maybe you've forgotten, but females are actually people!

HAMZA: Wow. You must be proper drunk, talking to me like...

MOSEY: Hamza. Are you gay?

HAMZA: Gay?

MOSEY: You heard me.

HAMZA: Am I gay?

MOSEY: Well are you gay?

HAMZA: Do I look like I'm gay?

MOSEY: Well, you sound it. 'Do I look like I'm gay' is a pretty gay thing to ask, wouldn't you say?

HAMZA: Would it be a problem if I was?

MOSEY: I think it might be for you. I think it super-might be, actually. I think you've got issues. But who cares what I think? Or what anyone thinks? Or feels?

MOSEY grabs HAMZA's drink and necks it.

MOSEY: (CONT'D) We're all just pussies, right?

HAMZA: Have you gone mad?

MOSEY: You tell me.

HAMZA: Are you having some kind of psychological melt-down?

MOSEY: You tell me.

HAMZA: Are you experiencing suicidal tendencies?

MOSEY: You tell...

HAMZA: No, actually – you tell me! 'Cause I'm seriously concerned for your physical and emotional well-being right now.

MOSEY: That's right, go on, call me gay. Call me confused. Call me the one who's projecting. Kick off ridiculous unnecessary arguments – fine with me – as long as you realise I'm not judging you. That I care about you. That I love you – no homo – and I mean no homo in a totally non-caveman, non-homophobic way – anyway, I'm just saying that I love you, mate – bruv – like family. And that if you were gay, I'd be here for you. Like I know you'd be here ...for me.

RYOKO: You don't have to kiss her, Mosey.

MOSEY makes a move towards SUMMER. RYOKO steps in his way.

RYOKO: (CONT'D) Bruv, it's okay...

MOSEY snatches RYOKO'S drink, drinks it down in one. Hands back the empty, marches round RYOKO then straight towards SUMMER. He thrusts her drink at her.

SUMMER: My hero!

SUMMER takes the drink and kisses MOSEY – a quick peck.

MOSEY: Oh my God!

JACK: Steady on, mate!

SUMMER: Thank you! I am too thirsty, but I couldn't stop dancing!

MOSEY: I'm gay. (*To SUMMER*) I'm gay!!

SUMMER: I know! (*Throwing her arms round his neck*) Isn't it amazing?

MOSEY gives SUMMER a big impulsive drunken kiss. The music surges... MOSEY comes up for air.

MOSEY: Oh my God. Summer ...I'm gay!

MOSEY kisses SUMMER again.

MOSEY: (CONT'D) I feel nothing! Nothing. Except gay. (*kiss*) Gayer... (*kiss*) Gayer! The more I kiss you, the gayer I get. No offence. Your lips are soft and lovely and even fun. But they're not his lips. Even though I've never kissed his lips. I know they're not his lips and so they're just lips. (*beat*) You know?

MOSEY looks at the BOYS all staring.

MOSEY: (CONT'D) You knew?

MOSEY walks unsteadily to look RYOKO in the face.

MOSEY: (CONT'D) You knew?

MOSEY bolts away.

RYOKO: Mosey!!!

RYOKO starts after him. Pauses to look back at JACK and HAMZA.

HAMZA: You'll be cool.

*HAMZA and JACK watch as RYOKO goes off after MOSEY.
When they turn back, SUMMER is gone.*

HAMZA: (CONT'D) Shit.

JACK: Summer!!!!

They exit.

ENTER MOSEY, drunk. Enter RYOKO. Silence.

MOSEY: Okay. Shall I start you off? You think I'm brave.

RYOKO: That's not it.

MOSEY: You're proud of me.

RYOKO: Yeah, but that's not it.

MOSEY: It doesn't make any difference. I'm still your boy – as in your bruv.

RYOKO: It was just... I'd never really noticed how quaint the G word is. You know? It just sounded so old-fashioned. I suppose. I don't know. I was called that in school a lot and it never sounded right. And now that it is – technically – right. It's still... quaint. But it's growing on me. (*beat*) I never knew. I just sort of... hoped. Now that's really corny, ain't it?

MOSEY: Maybe. I dunno. I guess it's complicated. I thought you liked pussies?

RYOKO: On the right person. I'm not too into minor details,

really, truth be told.

Silence.

MOSEY: Just 'cause we're unofficially gays now, don't mean we're not still queers.

RYOKO: I never liked that word either before.

MOSEY: The Q word?

RYOKO: Like the N word, there was a whip in there. Always made me flinch. But maybe it's time to stop being concerned about what people call us...

RYOKO moves closer to MOSEY...

MOSEY: Maybe it's time to start focusing on what we call ourselves.

MOSEY gets closer to RYOKO...

RYOKO: Explore our options...

MOSEY: ...After all there's never been a better time to be gay...

They lean in....

RYOKO: ...Or queer...

MOSEY: ...Or whatever...

...and just as they are about to kiss, they hear...

JOAN: (OFFSTAGE) I'd rather be a queer bitch than a straight dog any day, you dumb stupid caveman!

JOAN helps JUSTINE on. JUSTINE'S head is bleeding a little. JOAN is yelling at whoever is behind them.

JOAN: (CONT'D) Yeah, that's us, you messed-up knuckle-dragging missing-goddam-link – a pair of bitches! Just like your sister, just like your mama, just like every other woman with a functioning cortex that ever turned you down! Disgusting right? Two women minding their own business, living their existences, two women who do not need you! Who do not even know you're alive! Well, get used to it, Lil' Bow-Wow, 'cause that's gonna be your frickin' life!
God, I hate when they bring out the ghetto in me. Or maybe I love it, I don't know. I just don't want to despise anybody. But they make it so...
(*to JUSTINE*)
Shit, you're bleeding! (*tending to JUSTINE*) God, men can be ridiculous. Assholes...
(*yelling off*)
ASSHOLES! This is London, goddamit! Like nobody's ever seen two women dance together before...

JUSTINE: Not like us.

JOAN: (*trying to smile*) We did get a little close, didn't we?

JUSTINE: I mean not like me.

JOAN: Justine....

JUSTINE: You really think this a lesbian thing? Or a racism-thing? Does this happen when you're with other friends? Or when it's just you? You know, I've never wanted to blend in before.

JOAN: Why the hell should you?

JUSTINE: Why shouldn't I? Don't I have the right to wish I could walk down the street without either lowering my head, or forcing myself to stare every passing man in the eye? Don't I have the right to want to keep the people I care about alive?

JOAN: Doesn't everybody? You know what, screw it, we need to call the cops. Where's your phone? Did you lose it?

JUSTINE: I don't have it with me.

JOAN: Dammit. Both too cool for our own damn good.

JUSTINE: I haven't had a phone in five years. Since I lost my job and my flat and my sense of direction and went walk-about. I say walkabout 'cause it's so hard to say homeless. I've been homeless, Joan. I've been living in supported housing for the last eight months, on the streets before that, on friends' sofas and floors before that. I've always attracted the wrong things. Wrong people, wrong dramas, wrong drugs, wrong attention. That's what you were dancing with. That's what you dressed up for. That's what you kissed.

JOAN: Excuse me. I thought this wasn't a workshop?

JUSTINE: Well....

91

JOAN: 'Cause girlfriend, you are a lot of work.

JUSTINE: Too much work?

JOAN: You tell me.

JUSTINE: You can say it. Too much work for a girlfriend.

JOAN: Okay. How did we get here?

JUSTINE: I've always been here. This is where I live. This is it.

JOAN: Do you really believe that?

JUSTINE: We can't all live in happy-clappy Oprah world, you
    know. Using our oppression as food and fuel. Effortlessly
    juggling all the isms to build a global brand. Some of us are
    just hopelessly English. Some of us live in shit-holes filled
    with furniture found in skips. Some of us live life sandwich
    by sandwich. Failure by failure. Some of us are still learning
    to look after ourselves, how can we hope to look after
    anyone else?? Some of us are beyond broke – we're
    unfixable.

JOAN: Happy-clappy Oprah? Is that what you see?

JUSTINE: Isn't that what you want everyone to see?

JOAN: Not everyone.

 JOAN holds out a hand.

JOAN: (CONT'D) Show me where you live.

JUSTINE doesn't move.

JOAN: (CONT'D) I'll show you mine if you show me yours.

JUSTINE looks away.

JUSTINE: I can't. I don't want to let you down.

JOAN: Then don't.
Justine.... Justine.

JUSTINE: I know I'm pathetic but I don't know if I'm strong
enough to give them one more reason to hate me.

JOAN: ...Okay.... Okay.

JOAN walks away.

JUSTINE: Wow, that was quick. Even for me.

*MOSEY goes over to JUSTINE, puts an arm around her
shoulders. RYOKO watches awkwardly as JUSTINE rests her
head against MOSEY for a moment.*

JUSTINE: (CONT'D) Thank you for not loving me.

MOSEY: Justine.

JUSTINE: At least you spared me that. They never tell you, do
they? All those song and sonnets, yet no one tells you. It's
like someone says 'Hey, look outside.' And you go to the
window and there's a big shiny car at the kerb with a great
bow round it and you can't believe it, they're giving you a
car! You run outside barefoot, jump in, and you're wide-

eyed and breathless in the driver's seat just like Mummy or Daddy. Practically a grown up. Liberated. The world is your infinite oyster. And you turn the key and, even though you stall once or twice, you persevere and you pull out in the traffic and off you go. Cruising. Showing off. Look at me behind the wheel of my great big shiny car. And then there's petrol. And the insurance. And road tax and parking tickets and speeding fines and rear end shunts that only make a tiny dent but cost a fortune to fix and learning the Highway Code and parallel parking and MOT's and residents' permits. And the car's not even new, the 'one careful owner' ran it into the ground and it never really ran properly in the first place. But it was a car. With a ribbon round it. And so you didn't care. Until the day you found yourself in the middle of some cold dark wet nowhere waiting for roadside assistance to jump-start or tow your piece of junk. And it dawns on you what you thought was a gift has just been a money pit. Swallowing every penny you've got. What you thought was independence, is a dead weight. What you thought was a bundle of treats is yet another full-time job, when you pour everything you earn into something that never worked properly in the first place.
(*beat*)
Thanks. At least you spared me that.

JUSTINE starts to curl up in the grass, MOSEY starts to move away.

MOSEY: Are you okay?

JUSTINE: I usually am in the end.

MOSEY hovers, torn. RYOKO stands beside him watching JUSTINE. With cautious compulsion, their hands gradually find each other, until they are just about holding hands...

ENTER JACK.

RYOKO and MOSEY leap apart.

JACK: SUMMER! This is getting silly now... SUMMER!

MOSEY: We'll spread out.

JACK: If you find her, no kissing, though alright? For a gay guy, you kiss girls way too much, mate. SUMMER!

MOSEY: I'll go this way, yeah.

RYOKO: I'll go this way...?

They are looking at each other. Uncertain of commitment.

MOSEY: In a bit yeah?

RYOKO: Yeah, bruv.
Summer!

MOSEY: Summer!!!!

MOSEY and RYOKO exit.

JUSTINE starts to leave. Enter SUMMER drunk and dancing. She speaks to a member of the audience.

SUMMER: Hello. I'm Summer and I'm a Filipina... which means from the Philippines... and I am ever so slightly drunk. Sorry, I'm a British lady now. I'm piddly... no... tiddly.

I'm pissed. I'm rrrrrrrat-arsed! My lovely friends – they've been buying me drinks all evening. And now it's my shit... oops pardon, my 'shout', but I have no pockets and no purse and no pennies or pounds. So I was going to steal your drink and share it. But that's rude. And I'm not rude. I'm a good girl from a good family, and you look rich and kind, so I'm asking first if I can steal your drink, please? (*taking the drink*)
Thank you!

ENTER HAMZA

HAMZA: Whoa!!! Let's just put that back, shall we? Sorry about my friend, she's new. (*To SUMMER*) What the hell are you doing?

SUMMER: I'm being a cheeky London girl!

HAMZA: You gotta be careful, London girl. This city ain't as polite as in the films. Okay, let's go, before it all kicks off and you get a brother in trouble. I found her! You lot!

SUMMER: Is this our date?

HAMZA: No, it's Mosey's date, still.

SUMMER: Mosey's sweet. And gay! Isn't that cute?

HAMZA: Is it? Yeah, it's cute.

Trying to herd SUMMER, HAMZA is forced to take her hand.

SUMMER: That's why he kissed me! And the more he kissed me the gayer he got! Mosey's sweet. But he's not my favourite! That's why I'm glad it was you who found me.

HAMZA: Oh yeah?

SUMMER: (*whispers*) 'Cause you're my favourite. (*yells*) Hamza's my favourite!

HAMZA: Yeah, right.

SUMMER: Yeah, right! Because you don't like me.

HAMZA: You what?

SUMMER: All the others think they like me just because I look pretty. You don't like me 'cause you don't know me and you're honest. I like that. Thank you.

HAMZA: You're... Welcome?

SUMMER: You don't pretend to be interested. Like Ryoko, only asking questions he wanted to answer himself. He was nice though. But he's gay too. All the good guys are gay.

HAMZA: So they say. I'm sorry I called you a bitch.

SUMMER: That's just the way you talk.

HAMZA: Exactly. I don't actually think you're a bitch, though.

SUMMER: Maybe I am. Sometimes. Is that so terrible? Am I embarrassing you?

HAMZA: No. Yeah. Dunno.

SUMMER: Can I kiss you, please?

HAMZA: What for?

SUMMER: I want to get closer to those pretty eyes.

HAMZA: Our date's tomorrow.

SUMMER: What if I can't wait?

HAMZA: I still don't know nothing about you.

SUMMER: (*Moving closer*) My name is Summer Sanchez.
  Middle name Amihan... It means north-east wind.
  (*moves closer*)
  Tomorrow I'm 25 years old. Born in a summer day with a gentle...

HAMZA/SUMMER: ...north-east breeze...

HAMZA: ...I get it...

SUMMER: In school my favourite subjects were fashion and physics.

HAMZA: Okay.

SUMMER: My favourite colours are aquamarine and cherry red. My favourite song is Try a Little Tenderness. My favourite movie is Close Encounters of the First Kind.

They are close now.

SUMMER: (CONT'D) Are you getting all this?

HAMZA: Summer Amihan Sanchez, August 10th 1992, fashion and physics, aquamarine, cherry red, Try a Little Tenderness, Close Encounters of the Third Kind.

SUMMER: What's your favourite song?

HAMZA: Here Comes the Sun, by the Beatles.

SUMMER: Favourite movie?

HAMZA: Moonlight.

SUMMER kisses HAMZA.

And in the moon they are mirrored. A huge kiss.

JACK: (OFFSTAGE) Summer!

As JACK runs on, HAMZA leaps away from SUMMER. JACK looks at them, uncertain of what he thinks he's seen.

JACK: (CONT'D) You alright?

MOSEY: (O.S.) Summer!!!!

JACK: (*Eyes on HAMZA*) Over here!

RYOKO runs on, swiftly joined by MOSEY.

MOSEY: There you are! Thought I'd scared you off.

SUMMER throws her arms around each boy in turn.

SUMMER: Heyyyyy, Mosey! Hey Ryoko! Hey Jacky!!!

JACK: Jack.

SUMMER: Jack, Jack Handsome Captain Jack. The sun called and said she wants her sunshine back!

JACK doesn't react.

RYOKO: You alright, Jack?

JACK: Yeah.

SUMMER: What Jack needs... is a drink! We must steal him one!
(*rushing off*)
Excuse me thank you! Can I steal your drink, please?

RYOKO and MOSEY go after her.

RYOKO: Whooah!

MOSEY: Steady on, trouble!

JACK: I thought you didn't like her.

HAMZA: I didn't. That's why she kissed me.

JACK: Oh, of course, I get it now! She kissed you 'cause she's a bitch.

HAMZA: She's not a bitch.

JACK: Oh, she's not a bitch now?

HAMZA: Bitch doesn't always mean 'bitch'. Not in that way.

That's just how I talk. Sometimes.

JACK: And what are you? Don't tell me... a mate? A brother? Family?

HAMZA: I'm sorry.

JACK: Yeah. That's about right.

JACK walks off.

HAMZA alone.

JACK comes back.

JACK: (CONT'D) Do you like her?

HAMZA: Obviously, I...

JACK: Don't bullshit me, mate. Do you like her? Did you want to kiss her?

HAMZA: No.

JACK: Where are you taking her?

HAMZA: Taking her?

JACK: Tomorrow on your date.

HAMZA: Nowhere.

JACK: Nowhere? You're cancelling the date? Not for me.

HAMZA: There was never no date, bruv! You know me, I'm a wasteman and proud! What my mum – if she was still talking to me – would call a scrub! That's me, fam! Shame-lessly slick! I step to 'em, give 'em a whiff of my sweet breath and cologne, gold-standard chirpse 'em, then leave 'em twisting in the wind waiting for their smartphone to light up, until the moment they finally realise that they're just numbers in my pocket. No rings, no beeps, no buzzes on WhatsApp. I am done and I am dusted. All trailer, no film, that's Hamza. And I ain't even guilty or feeling no kind of way, 'cause mans is <u>busy</u> fam! I ain't got time for smiling in no gyal's eyes and acting all semi-sincere over a whole meal that's eating up my Nando's loyalty points. I ain't got time for cryptic texting and cutesy manipulative, passive-aggressive emoticons. I ain't got time for remembering birthdays, anniversaries or the colour of some girl's contact lenses. And neither have you, playa! We got runnings to run. Paper to make. Winter's coming! And at this latitude, winter is long! So no I ain't going on no date. I'm otherwise engaged. To myself!

JACK: You're actually planning to stand up Summer? You... bounder!

HAMZA: You're probably lucky I don't know what that means.

JACK: You can't just leave her standing there waiting for you. Who does that?

HAMZA: Looks like you're about to find out.

JACK: Fine. Then I guess I'll just have to take her out again, won't I?

HAMZA: Wow, you just can't suffer enough, can, you? Fine. Whatever. She's all yours.

JACK: No, mate, she's not all mine. Yet.

HAMZA: I'm not standing in your way. I wish you luck and love. You deserve it.

JACK: Oh, I get it! You'd love that, wouldn't you? To have her talking to someone else and wondering where you are and how you are and if you're okay. No mate, we'll not be playing that game thank you kindly sir.

HAMZA: What the fizzle is your problem now? You got your second chance. You can be her knight in shining armour! What more do you want?

JACK: I want Summer.

HAMZA: What more can I do about it?

JACK: Turn up.

HAMZA: You what?

JACK: Turn up. Take her on a date. The worst date in the history of dates. Step on her feet, call her the wrong name, fart, tell racist jokes... you can crash the car... and let me rescue her.

HAMZA: You're out of your mind.

JACK: I am mate. I'm all hers. Do this for me. Please. I'm begging you, fam.

MOSEY: (O.S.) Over here!

RYOKO: (O.S.) Mosey?

MOSEY: She's over here!

We hear SUMMER laughing OFFSTAGE.

MOSEY: (CONT'D) Help!

JACK: I'm begging you.

JACK runs off.

HAMZA goes over to JUSTINE. Sits beside her.

HAMZA: You were right. Boys can be dicks.

JUSTINE: That's not what I said. Technically.
  You were right. Women are work.

HAMZA: That wasn't actually me, but still...

JUSTINE: Women are a full time job.

HAMZA: Someone been giving you a hard time?

JUSTINE: Worse. I am the hard time.

HAMZA: Ah.

JUSTINE: You know what I'm like. What was the phrase? I
  think it meant high-maintenance.

HAMZA: Long.

JUSTINE: Long. I'm long, man.

HAMZA: To be fair, people are long in general.

JUSTINE: I don't want to be though. I want to be... (*sighs*) ...fun. I was fun when I was four. Running round with my hair in my eyes naked at the paddling pool. No list of regulations. No lane to stay in. I was fun.

HAMZA: I think you're fun now. Deep down.

JUSTINE: I'm not really though, am I? I'm long.

HAMZA: Long is good. When it's the right kind. You gotta be a bit complicated. No one wants just a cover with no book inside.

JUSTINE: Okay.

HAMZA: Well , do you want someone who's just fun? Or do you want someone with levels?

JUSTINE: Levels are appealing, I suppose.

HAMZA: It's the levels that keep you coming back ain't it?

JUSTINE: Like video games?

HAMZA: Exactly.

JUSTINE: Well, I'm Grand Theft Auto uncensored. Oh my God, it's just a date. With someone beautiful. ...Why's it so scary?

People do them all the time. You've been on how many dates times infinity?

Silence.

JUSTINE: (CONT'D) You are joking..? Oh my gosh! Well, at least you'll be authentically crap at it. Who knew we had so much in common? So where are you taking her?

HAMZA: I dunno.

JUSTINE: You don't know? You must have thought about it.

HAMZA: I dunno.

JUSTINE: You were going to bottle out of it? You were genuinely intending to stand her up and leave her waiting?

HAMZA: I dunno, alright? I dunno! Where am I supposed to take a girl like that? Where's good enough? Where's worthy? A flippin' food-bank? I wasn't thinking about it. What is there to think about? It's like death. You know it's coming, but what's the point in making plans?

JUSTINE: Oh my double gosh, you're actually worse than me. I am so so happy.

HAMZA: It's all part of the service.

JUSTINE: Regent's Park? If you detour round the part near the zoo you can sometimes see the heads of the giraffes.

HAMZA: Ryoko already done that one on the way to Primrose Hill.

JUSTINE: British Museum's free. Tate's Free. Royal Academy
of Arts free.

HAMZA: Are these all ideas for the rubbish date option? If so,
they're brilliant.

JUSTINE: What can I say? I'm gifted. So art is 'moist' then?
Well, maybe it is. Maybe I like moist.

HAMZA: (*Almost blushing*) Hush man! (*shyly*) S'gotta be the
Tate Modern, ain't it? Open late on a Friday. Amazing
architecture... There's the walk over the pedestrian bridge
from Saint Paul's as the sun goes down.... all the blue lights
in the trees. What?

JUSTINE: Oh my triple gosh... Hamza's a romantic!

HAMZA: Oh man! I'm 20 years old! I ain't got time to get
caught up in all that. I ain't responsible. I can't be trusted.
I'll hurt someone.

HAMZA looks away.

JUSTINE: Oh, my... Okay, I'm losing count now... A movie
won't hurt her. Open air screening in the Scoop or Hyde
Park or...

HAMZA: A rooftop overlooking the rooftop cinema.

They sit together and enact it all.

JUSTINE: Deckchairs side by side... and shoulders lightly
touching... She's got flowers in her lap you...

HAMZA: ...grew specially for her...

JUSTINE: You've got popcorn in your lap you...

HAMZA: Paid for. Popcorn I paid for. It can happen.

JUSTINE: It's happening. And there you are together looking at the screen...

HAMZA: ...lost in everything

JUSTINE: Until you realise the screen is looking back at you and you don't know where the film ends... and where life begins...

HAMZA: ...we are the movie...

JUSTINE: ...and the movie is us. And just for a couple of hours...

HAMZA: ...Everything is beautiful.

UP ON THE SCREEN we see SUMMER and HAMZA on a date... Watching the skateboarders on the SOUTH BANK, Going across the river on the Greenwich cable-car.

This becomes JOAN and JUSTINE sunning themselves on an inner city beach, sharing Mr Whippy ice-creams... JUSTINE'S sleepy head resting on JOAN's shoulder on the DLR. Whizzing together down the OLYMPIC PARK SLIDE.

Suddenly JOAN enters. JUSTINE jumps up.

JUSTINE: Joan!

HAMZA: It's not what it looks like.

JOAN: I know that, big boy, don't flatter yourself.
(*To JUSTINE*) I live in my car. Okay? I live in my goddam car. Sleep in it, eat in it. Hold business meetings in it. Okay? I shower at the leisure centre. Fix my hair with straighteners plugged into the cigarette lighter. Women all over the world do it every day, it's no big deal, I'll survive it and move on. Now show me where you live. Please.

JUSTINE: Well, why didn't you just say that in the first place?

JOAN: Well, you seemed so disgusted with your little studio, I thought Jesus, what's she gonna say when she sees I live in a damn car?

JUSTINE: Is it air-conditioned?

JOAN: Bitch please.

JUSTINE: Oh, thank God! Let's go. I live in Canning Town. (*as she goes*) Don't look like that!

JOAN: Did I say anything?

HAMZA left alone. Looks up at the screen.

Footage of JUSTINE and JOAN holding hands in the market-place becomes HAMZA and SUMMER lying in the long grass together. Looking up at the sky.

MUSIC

SUNRISE

OLYMPIC PARK

JACK & MOSEY watch SUMMER waiting in a pretty dress.

JACK: He'll turn up. No man worth bothering with would fail to turn up for you.

MOSEY and RYOKO drop to the ground and sit with them. They wait.

JACK: (CONT'D) Trust me, Hamza's a good bloke. He'll be here.

Silence.

JACK: (CONT'D) Okay, I'm gonna kill him.

RYOKO: Men are such bastards.

MOSEY: Thanks.

RYOKO: Well we are. Sorry, Summer.

SUMMER: Sorry, did you say something?

BOYS exchange looks.

SUMMER: (CONT'D) Forgive me, I am very rude. I will make it up to you. I'm taking you on a date.

RYOKO: A date?

MOSEY: Taking who?

JACK: Taking me?

BOYS: You can't do that/That's not the deal/Babe, that's really not on...

SUMMER: Please...

The BOYS fall silent.

SUMMER: (CONT'D) ...Do not embarrass me more. I am taking you on a date.

HAMZA: Oi! That's my line.

HAMZA arrives. Dressed up, but somewhat dishevelled.

Silence.

HAMZA: (CONT'D) Wassup.

JACK: 'Wassup'? You're an hour late, mate.

HAMZA: Yeah.

JACK: That's all you got to say for yourself? State of you. You look out of it.

Out of SUMMER's eye-line, JACK gives HAMZA the thumbs up.

HAMZA: Story of my life. (*beat*) But here I am. What's left of me. (*to SUMMER*) May I say, you look particularly doable this afternoon, Summer babe.

SUMMER: 'Doable'? What is doable, please?

JACK: Pretty. Doable means you look especially...

HAMZA: Shaggable. Doable means shaggable. Hot. Which is bollocks. It's true but it's bollocks. How you actually look is how you always look – which is beautiful.

SUMMER: Thank you.

HAMZA: Which is why I act stupid round you and say stupid shit. Because you're beautiful.

JACK: Right, so, where you taking her then?

HAMZA: Back to mine.

JACK: You what?

HAMZA: (*indicating the park*) These weeds are my mattress. These clouds are my ceiling. That horizon is my walls. This view of the city is my TV. Fell out with my family, with the education system, with every boss I've ever tried to have. No one can stand to be around me – and I've never wanted to be around anyone else – 'cept for these three mugs, and they get on my nerves – until you. I want to be around you. And I ain't got a car to sleep in or a room in a halfway house. I ain't got a pot to piss in or a box to shit in or a single job prospect or even a stable brain. All I've got is this grass, this sky, this view and a mad feeling for some bird named Summer. Who I know nothing about and want to know everything about and don't know how to ask. I know this is the worst non-date ever. I never thought I'd ever be in love. I didn't know how to. I had no plan except stay away. But I couldn't even do that right. And here I am. At the mercy of beauty. And whatever you decide, I will do. Because you're my family, you're my education. You're the boss.

JACK: You bastard! You evil, selfish, duplicitous, sly bastard.

HAMZA: Ain't sly and duplicithingy the same word?

JACK: Bastard!

JACK whacks HAMZA with his bouquet.

JACK: (CONT'D) Bastard! Bastard!

HAMZA: Oh, bruv, come on...

SUMMER: Jack, what are you doing?!!

JACK: Go on defend him! After he just told you to your face that he does not know how to love you.

MOSEY: Jack, you need to calm down, mate.

JACK: None of these losers have a clue how to love you. Or treat you.

MOSEY: Oi, steady on!

RYOKO: Why you dragging us into it?

JACK: You're just a game to them. But not to me.

HAMZA: It was your idea, weren't it?

JACK: What have you been smoking, geezer? You really think we would have let all of you move in with us?

MOSEY: Yeah, who'd be mug enough to be that kind of mate.

SUMMER: Move in with us where?

JACK: Your place. Obviously I wouldn't have let 'em.

SUMMER: My place?

JACK: Where you live.

Silence.

JACK: (CONT'D) You are joking...? Oh, for crying out... Is this park just full of homeless street trash?

SUMMER: Street trash?

JACK: Not you. I mean... you know what I mean.

SUMMER: Not everyone who is homeless lives on the street.

JACK: Oh, right. So who do you stay with then?

SUMMER: I have cousins. Friends.

RYOKO: So you're like sofa surfing, then?

MOSEY: Going from house to house.

SUMMER: Until I find work, yes. It is hard.

HAMZA: Tell me about it.

JACK: Like you've been looking for a job, mate. Do me a favour.

HAMZA: Where do you think I've been all morning?

JACK: Oh, so that was the plan is it? Get yourself the job, the flat and the girl all in one brilliant morning and bye-bye band of brothers. You know what? You two deserve each other. You're both liars.

SUMMER: When did I lie, please?

JACK: When did you mention that you're homeless?

SUMMER: When did you ask me?

JACK: Never.

Pause.

SUMMER: Never.

JACK goes over and fetches his sleeping bag and clock from their hiding place.

MOSEY: Where you going? Jack....

JACK: You know I don't know where I'm going! I'm just going! I get it. I'm a shit person and shit friend, total waste of space. I get it.

HAMZA: Mate...

JACK: Haven't you got enough? Can't you even let me have my bitterness? Are you so determined to have everything worth having round here that you need my love too? Do you really need me to swallow everything and hold it down and stand around smiling good on you mate if it goes your way, or give you my shoulder to drench if she decides she's not so sweet on you when she's sober. You're not my brother. You are not duty-bound to forgive me. You've known me for one year.

HAMZA: Yeah, but what a year.

JACK: Just let me go, yeah. Let me go?

HAMZA: Okay. But only because I care about you.

JACK: I know you do. You bastard.

JACK leaves.

HAMZA: (*affectionate*) ...Mug.

SUMMER starts to leave.

HAMZA: (CONT'D) Where you going?

SUMMER: We're not going to just let him walk away.

HAMZA: Aren't we?

SUMMER: That's not what family does.

HAMZA: Family? You're family now?

SUMMER: Of course.

SUMMER is gone. HAMZA follows.

HAMZA: So you're Jack's sister...? Or sister-in-law?

SUMMER: Jack!

HAMZA: Jack, man! Jack, mate! Jack, bruv!
(*OFFSTAGE*)
Ey, wait up bro!

MOSEY & RYOKO left alone.

THE SUN is going into an ECLIPSE.

RYOKO: Whoa.

MOSEY: Wow.

RYOKO: Love is a lot. All that worrying about what you look like and sound like and smell like.

MOSEY: Wondering where they are, and what they're doing...

RYOKO: ...and whether they're thinking about you...

MOSEY: Just a great big ego bomb.

RYOKO: Making you act like a jealous obsessive clingy junkie stalker...

MOSEY: ...That forgets that half your mates even exist and drives the other half away with stomach churning baby-talk

and embarrassing public snogs.

RYOKO: And expensive, man!

MOSEY: Oh my gosh, love costs a bloody fortune!

RYOKO: Love is jokes.

MOSEY: All that tedious getting to know each other.

RYOKO: All that time-consuming spooning and cuddling.

MOSEY: All those compliments.

RYOKO: All those kisses.

MOSEY: All those dreams.

RYOKO: All that optimism.

MOSEY: All those plans.

RYOKO moves closer to MOSEY.

RYOKO: It's a mystery why anyone even bothers.

MOSEY moves closer to RYOKO.

MOSEY: They must be on something.

RYOKO: They must be deluded.

MOSEY: They must be totally...

RYOKO: ...out of their...

MOSEY: ...minds.

RYOKO and MOSEY kiss.

FULL ECLIPSE

LIGHTS UP on JUSTINE and JOAN slow-dancing in the rain.

JUSTINE: Some words are timeless. They never grow old, part of every language since our infant days, when everything is new and nothing is strange.

JOAN: Some moves are effortless, they've been part of us since we were brave and mighty amoebas separating and blending the way raindrops do, all adventure and no fear.

JUSTINE: All possibility and no limits.

JOAN: All instinct and no calculation.

JUSTINE: Making shapes.

JOAN: Making futures.

JUSTINE: Making worlds within worlds.

JOAN: Dreams within dreams

JUSTINE: Homes within homes.

JOAN: And just for a little while...

JUSTINE: ...everything is beautiful.

END

Also available from Team Angelica Publishing

'Reasons to Live' by Rikki Beadle-Blair
'What I Learned Today' by Rikki Beadle-Blair

'Faggamuffin' by John R Gordon
'Colour Scheme' by John R Gordon
'Souljah' by John R Gordon

'Fairytales for Lost Children' by Diriye Osman

'Black & Gay in the UK – an anthology' edited by John R
Gordon & Rikki Beadle-Blair

'More Than – the Person Behind the Label' edited by
Gemma Van Praagh

'Tiny Pieces of Skull' by Roz Kaveney

'Slap' by Alexis Gregory'

'Custody' by Tom Wainwright

Fimí sílẹ̀ Forever by Nnanna Ikpo

Lightning Source UK Ltd.
Milton Keynes UK
UKOW01f0106060717
304755UK00004B/18/P